With Love
to Gill.

16/5/20

THE THIRD VISION

by

Giovanna
O'HALLORAN-BINDI

Story, Author photograph, Cover Design & Illustrations all Copyright ©2019

by Giovanna O'Halloran-Bindi

First Published: 2019

English translation & Editing by Noel O'Halloran-Bindi

"Wind blows. Your helpful breezes blow away Evil. You are the medicine of all this world – the messenger of the Gods"

Veda RVX, 137,3

CONTENTS

INTRODUCTION

Chapter 1 - LUNIA – *By the window.*

Chapter 2 - ALEX – *The Call*

Chapter 3 - LUNIA – *The Mysterious Object*

Chapter 4 - ALEX – *The Little Robot*

Chapter 5 - LUNIA – *The Intruder*

Chapter 6 - ALEX – *The Delivery*

Chapter 7 - LUNIA – *The Message*

Chapter 8 - ALEX – *The Picture*

Chapter 9 - LUNIA – *Arriving in Egypt*

Chapter 10 - ALEX – *Faiia's Declaration*

Chapter 11 - LUNIA – *The Second Message*

Chapter 12 - ALEX – *Moving to Luxor*

Chapter 13 - LUNIA – *The Escape*

Chapter 14 - ALEX & LUNIA – *The Meeting*

Chapter 15 - ALEX & LUNIA - *Italy*

Chapter 16 - THE TWO WOMEN – *The Esoteric Egyptian Society*

Chapter 17 - FRIAR SUN – *The Alchemy of the Spirit*

Chapter 18 - THE MASURITI – *The Darkening*

Chapter 19 - LUNIA – *No Escape*

Chapter 20 - ALEX – *Returning to Egypt*

Chapter 21 - LUNIA – *The Revelation*

Chapter 22 - ALEX – *Prince Charming*

Chapter 23 - DENDRA TEMPLE – *The Secret Door*

Chapter 24 - ESOTERIC SCIENCE – *The Alchemy of the Spirit*

Chapter 25 - THE THREE VISIONS – *The Line - The Circle – The Spiral*

Chapter 26 - THE BLACK MASURITI – *The Investigation*

Chapter 27 - THE SACRED PLACE – *Glastonbury, England*

Chapter 28 - THE INVESTIGATION – *The Orion Sect*

Chapter 29 - DENDRA – *Elizabeth*

Chapter 30 - LUNIA – *The Story*

THE AUTHOR – *Giovanna O'Halloran-Bindi*

Disclaimer

This is a work of fiction.

Names, characters, businesses, places, events, locales, and incidents are either the products of the author's imagination or used in a fictitious manner.

Any resemblance to actual persons, living or dead, or actual events is purely coincidental.

INTRODUCTION

This is Lunia's story, a young woman who dreams of escaping from her family and from the rest of the world that she observes through her window.

One day, she discovers a strange object, which brings her into contact with Alex, a young American archaeologist engaged in excavations of the Great Pyramid of Giza.

Together they discover that they have a surprising destiny reserved for them, as they adventure across Egypt, Italy and England whilst researching a precious oracle: the Key that opens a mystery for all human kind on Earth.

Fused between spirituality and thriller, their adventure blossoms into a rich scenario full of fantasy, which flows like a flooding river into the great sea of the Universe - with all of its secrets.

"We are not rigid separate things, but fluid elements in continuous vibration; like cells of the same blood, we are moving into the river of life, carrying with us nourishment for one body that encloses us all as pillars of the same temple."

'The Temple of Life' by Giovanna O'Halloran-Bindi ©2006

1

LUNIA

By the Window

Lunia was fifteen years old when she decided to begin to write her first diary *"I hate men that control women but mostly the women who let them be in control!"*

She had just finished arguing with her father yet again, and her mother had threatened to abandon the house once more. It had become a regular feature of Lunia's life and she was now growing very tired of the situation. It was always the same story with the same outcome: a lot of chaos for nothing because in the end her father still needs her mother and her mother cannot survive without him. Therefore everything always concludes without any solution being achieved and they each retreat into their comfortable cocoons once more.

She was repeatedly being told she was too young but now, at the age of twenty, she understood the world of adults and she didn't like it at all; especially when it was about gaining control of others. Any time any one of them tried to emerge in that way, she always had a strong feeling that began with disgust, then turned into deep compassion for the person who tried to dominate, who she knew, was going to fail and then fall into a deep sense of impotence and frustration.

It was a summer afternoon and there was silence, broken only by the sound of crickets between the trees. The sun was very high in the sky, which was misty white from the dampness and humidity that is so typical of a Mediterranean country during the summer. The landscape was characterised by dry vegetation. All around, the area was suffering from a drought and the dark burnt brown and yellows were reminiscent of the residue left behind after a fire.

That day Lunia was alone in the house. Outside there wasn't a breath of wind. She locked herself in her bedroom, lying down on the bed and allowing her dreams to drift across the ceiling, dreaming of the seaside and capturing in her imagination the sensation of the fresh sea breeze. Lunia was twenty but she felt older than her age. Maybe she had grown up too fast? On her face were the signs of having been burnt at an early age from hard experiences. She was the only child of a simple family, living and working in the countryside. Lunia was a young woman who often dreamed of rich adventures that would bring her far from home and the frustrations that her parents often make her feel: isolated, misunderstood and sometimes also sad. But thanks to her strong sense of creativity she could easily distract her mind through her imagination.

The big house she lived in with her parents was originally the home of her grandparents. It was where

Lunia was born and grew up and where love, in particular from her grandmother, had been suddenly and violently interrupted after a fatal accident which took away what represented the nest of her refuge.

The telling of stories beside the fireplace, and the delicious meals prepared with so much passion with thousands of recommendations on life and death which both the grandparents regularly delivered, had been taken away on that cursed day that saw her grandparents killed, when the tractor her grandfather was driving to plough the field, overturned.

She was just a teenager and she heard the screaming sound of the tractor engine suddenly rise up higher and higher. When she ran to the window she saw her poor grandparents crushed by the tractor, which seemed to be like some crazy beast, stamping on them both without any compassion. There was nothing anyone could do for the two old people: their life concluded in one moment. A moment that even after all these years still disturbed Lunia's mind and made her shudder anytime she heard the loud engine noise of a tractor nearby.

The empty space in the house, after the disappearance of her grandparents, could never be refilled and even the parents suffered greatly from the loss: isolating themselves to find comfort in their own separate worlds as communication between them became ever more argumentative. Lunia too found comfort in her own world of fantasy where she could recreate her ideal life in which she would enjoy the illusion of running away from reality.

That day she couldn't relax as usual, maybe because of the hot weather that was sticking her skin to the fresh linen bed sheet which her grandmother had bought and embroidered for her as a present for her fourteenth birthday. "Always the same presents" Lunia thought as she observed the regular floral handmade pattern that was bordering the cushion which surrounded her head. At that time she would have preferred a new bicycle or a beautiful brown leather jacket that she could show off in front of her mates: at fourteen it is still more important to appear than to be. Now she looks at the cushion with great fondness; happy to still possess something that reminds her, of her beautiful, loving grandmother.

In Italy it was a tradition for mothers and grandmothers to provide a list of items called 'Corredo' such as bed-sheets, towels and table cloths which were given as gifts for the home to female teenagers and stored in a cupboard for when they got married. In this way, when a woman found a husband all she needed to provide was the love.

But traditions are slowly being abandoned and the world is opening up like a wonderland where even the youngest can initiate adventure by taking their first faltering steps and occasionally triumph on what they gain from each new experience. What experience can cause a young woman to grow up fast in one giant step? Which traumatic experience if it's not a one way trip towards the unknown?...

She went over to the window, looking for fresh air to breathe but she found only heat from the high sun that was beaming through the glass like an oven, when she heard something that froze her blood…

2

ALEX

The Call

He was lying down, exhausted from the heat, in the shadow of the big pyramid. Alex Tarantino was a young American with Italian origins. He had just got his degree in archaeology and had begun the excavations one month before, after receiving the offer to work for mister Bajin, the owner of a company working for museums around Cairo that displayed pieces of high value archaeology.

This particular project was giving mister Bajin lots of problems because the law meant that every piece over two thousand years old belonged to the Egyptian government and therefore couldn't be retained by private companies. Bajin managed one of the biggest companies concerned with archaeologist's excavations in the area and he had no intention of sharing his chunk of the business with anyone who was bigger than him, including the government. To avoid problems which might risk shutting him down, he was paying very highly the government agents empowered to prosecute anyone appropriating antique artefacts without permission.

Alex accepted his first commissioned work directly from mister Bajin who was infamous for being someone who was happy to profit from young ex-students keen to get their first experience of work. The young archaeologist heard about mister Bajin and he didn't like what he was hearing, but he knew he couldn't begin his career without accepting the work and he was now in sole charge of the excavations within one of the rooms inside the big pyramid.

He always dreamed of one day discovering something sensational or at least very important, which could bring him notoriety and prestige within the world of archaeology. But the reason he loved this job was something deeper and more spiritual: to discover the secrets of the bigger mysteries of ancient Egypt and to learn to decipher the messages of what he regarded as a highly evolved people who had the knowledge and ability to build such enormous and technically perfect pyramids in a time which according to orthodox science, was around twelve thousand years before Christ.

Perfectly positioned architectural forms on Earth, the pyramids mirrored exactly the location of the stars in the constellation of Orion. Even the river Nile, bordering the three pyramids of Giza with its impetuous Sphinx, corresponded to the pattern of the Milky Way in the sky. What is hidden behind a mystery so great? What are the secrets that reveal such advanced techniques and such evolved knowledge? Who were the ancient Egyptians? Were they perhaps descendants from the mythical city of Atlantis or perhaps they even came from another planet? These and many other questions were what gave Alex his reasons to be there, and fired his obsession with the mysterious world the Egyptians had made and he swore to himself that one day he would discover their secrets, whatever the cost.

It was two o'clock in the afternoon. Alex had just taken a short break and had been lying down resting, when the radio transmitted a report that someone was looking for him. He wanted to switch it off using the excuse that the area he was in didn't have any reception but he reminded himself that even the smallest things with apparently no meaning could be very beneficial for his research.

"I'm Alex, who is speaking?" he spoke into the radio with the weary voice of someone who had recently woken up.

"Get ready for a nice surprise young man!" answered an older, heavier voice which sounded quite hoarse.

Alex became suddenly alert "Can I ask who is speaking?" he asked, somewhat intrigued and now fully awake to the agitation of such a strange message.

"I can't reveal my name at this moment Alex, but I want to help you to make an important discovery, one which I guarantee will be of great interest to you.

Something that will satisfy your curiosity and reveal many ancient Egyptian secrets. Go along the long corridor that takes you to the room with the gate and everything will become clear" directed the voice.

"Who is this?" repeated Alex but the connection ended suddenly by the caller switching off.

3

LUNIA

The Mysterious Object

An engine revs wildly, bringing back the memory of her grandparents death. A black range rover skids to a halt amongst the vineyards and a woman leaps out of the vehicle and then a man from the drivers side. They are standing in front of the vehicle shouting and gesturing violently at each other. At first Lunia thinks these two strange individuals are just having a lovers tiff when the man suddenly becomes very agitated and threatens the woman with a gun.

Lunia is frozen to the spot but can see that the woman is blonde with a slender and attractive build and that he is a tall, rugged looking man with a Middle Eastern appearance but it is too far away to identify them well. The woman recoils slowly backwards with her hands up as if to placate the man for long enough to get back into the car, which she does. The man waves the gun furiously around the head of the woman before grabbing the car door to slam it shut on her.

Just before the woman jumps into the car Lunia sees a strange luminous object fall to the ground from her hand, into the vegetation around. It is most likely something metal because it reflects the sunlight as it falls and it seemed like the woman had decided to get rid of it before the man noticed. "It must be something important" thought Lunia.

The man spins the range rovers wheels impatiently on the parched earth as he stamps on the accelerator, evidently very annoyed. Lunia watches as the vehicle shudders away violently like a crazed horse towards the horizon. She waits for the car to disappear completely and then goes out to look for the strange object in the area where she had seen it fall.

The house is surrounded by a large area of agricultural land. On the right side rows of still immature vineyards stretching out like a verdant river that disappears to the horizon behind a hill. It was precisely between those vineyards that she had seen, in the distance, the couple arguing.

She leaves the house, walking slowly and barefoot on the earth, which is still scorching from the sun. When she comes to the spot she looks down but finds nothing. Then her eyes catch sight of a strange twinkle nearby, stealing from between some green vineyard leaves. Her heart begins to beat strongly and she is thrilled and at the same time afraid by such a strange surprise. It seems almost impossible that this is happening to her, but it is, and the object is something she has never seen before in her life. As she picks it up from the hot dust she quickly gathers from its appearance that it is something precious but also something quite peculiar.

4

ALEX

The Little Robot

Alex stayed for a few moments with the radio in his hand since the man with the husky voice so abruptly hung up on him. Alex was confused and amused but also quite curious. Who could this man be? Why was he instructing him to go inside the great pyramid?

"Perhaps he was the resurrection of some mummified Pharaoh?" mused Alex to himself as he recalled the rasping hoarseness of the man's voice "or maybe it was just a practical joke being played on me by a colleague who was amusing himself after a hard days work?" The heat was causing them all to be driven crazy by some strange spirit of adventure. Alex was nevertheless fascinated that the caller had spoken directly about the room with the gate which happened to be the very area he was intent on exploring next. Confused, he decided to return to his work of exploring the maze of the pyramid.

On the way there Alex remembered that phone call he'd had to make to his boss mister Bajin when he'd first realised that the room with the gate was not going to be viable to reach. He'd known immediately that he would require some sophisticated robotic camera equipment to be able to penetrate the tiny tunnels with infrared beams and connect them up to a remote viewing screen on which transmitted images could be observed from the outside.

The equipment involved was highly expensive and usually financed by the 'Antiquities Affairs' department of the Egyptian government. Authority to use it was given only in very particular circumstances to companies involved in archaeological excavations due to its cost. The highly sophisticated use of such machines meant that they were protected by an insurance company who had already investigated their use and had found that mister Bajin's company seemed tied in to some unclear business practices involving possible false turnover, corruption and strange injections of what they believed might be 'dirty' money. All of this had not stopped Alex whose intentions had been driven by the extreme need for this precious tool.

He recalled that fateful telephone conversation with mister Bajin whose ample butt had been comfortably seated on his favourite swivel chair, were he always seemed to be smoking a cigarette and shouting down the phone to the rest of the world in a way that was very typical of that type of businessman; those who are lazy and actually do very little of the real work.

"Are you crazy?" had been Bajin's first yelled response. Faiia had heard him scream. She was his secretary and had been working for Bajin for about two years. Alex knew that Faiia was dreaming every day about leaving her boss and escaping with some money to Europe or America where she might be able to have an independent life and certainly a life less frustrating than hers was in Egypt.

Alex enjoyed chatting with her in an effort to recruit her as his ally hidden within Bajin's office. Alex also knew that she desperately needed to take a break from Bajin's screaming and that she was really tired of being the direct victim on whom her boss vented all his rage, using emotional blackmail and gestures of repressed violence intended to intimidate her and to atone somehow for his own inner guilt.

"I can't tolerate your absurd demands" Bajin shouted down the phone to Alex after a long pause that indicated there had been an insistent request from the young American. Faiia had sometimes seen Alex swoop into mister Bajin's office with the distressed air of someone who typically dreamed like her, in a vain attempt to escape from their everyday frustrations, and felt sympathy with him.

"I'll see what I can do but I'm promising nothing!" yelled Bajin finally: but another long delay had meant that the young American was again using his persuasive power very effectively.

Alex always knew how valuable his work was to Bajin and this allowed him to bargain very hard without risking his career. Faiia had breathed a sigh of relief that someone knew how to handle Bajin, and hoped that her 'American prince' would one day take her away with him and then she could finally reveal to him her unspoken passions.

"I need you to put pressure on the Authorities for this" demanded Alex "Let me have the camera by tonight and I'm sure I will raise your business success further than you can imagine with some sensational discoveries" he concluded dramatically, trying to doubly convince himself that his demands were both reasonable and urgent.

Mister Bajin repeated "For the umpteenth time, I do not promise anything – but I also can't risk this business closing for the cost of a trivial tool that maybe will not even give us the crumbs of a sensational discovery".

"Speak to you soon mister Bajin" finished Alex "I'll wait for your news as soon as possible and obviously I hope its positive."

"I hope so too, you young, reckless, ball breaker, otherwise we will meet again in Hell!" Bajin yelled slamming down the phone.

Mister Bajin had ended the communication in his usual brutal fashion, leaving Alex at the mercy of events that sometimes seemed irreparably intertwined with directions down a dead end road. But not long afterwards Alex had been pleasantly surprised by a return call from Bajin with very welcome news.

"I've secured the equipment you need to continue the work Alex" Bajin boasted.

"Thanks Bajin" Alex replied with genuine gratefulness "You won't be disappointed"

"I hope not. For *your* sake" Bajin added grumpily as he hung up.

5

LUNIA

The Intruder

As she picked up the object she noticed that it resembled a sophisticated ancient seal, reminiscent of precious artefacts that reminded her of something she'd seen during visits to the museum. The object was about seven centimetres long in the shape of a cross with a big loop at the top and it was decorated with beautifully embossed designs including tiny inlaid stones. Lunia greeted it with genuine surprise and carefully hid it underneath her shirt. Walking home in a hurry she had a sudden fear that there may already be someone out there who was spying on her.

When she arrived home she slammed the door behind her, almost as if to keep away the ghost voices inside, that already pursued her. She often heard an ominous and threatening voice that was intent on punishing her every time she did something wrong, or did something against the morals of her parents. It took possession of her, even when her parents were not present. Now she had something that clearly didn't belong to her and she was beginning to feel the arrival of guilt.

"What are you doing Lunia?" the voice interrogated "Put that object back where you found it or you will regret it bitterly!"

As she climbed the stairs Lunia was feeling afraid but also excited by that mixture of curiosity and the discovery of something totally new. Like so many young people, she decided to continue this adventure, defying her ghosts by banishing them to the shadows of the long night; a night that would close one chapter of her life and open up a new one!

Before figuring out where to start, Lunia opened her book of Veda, to which she often returned whenever she felt the need for wise counsel or to overcome difficult situations. She allowed one page to randomly speak out to her:

"What is done in the darkness of the night has for witnesses the stars; guardian spectators of the Universal Order. Heaven and Earth can meet only on the horizon, light and darkness only in the twilight of the morning or the evening; there is no singing without a corresponding verse, neither without its melody." Raimon Pannikar – Veda

She understood then that what she was getting involved in was inevitable. She would have no choice but to go down this untrodden route and continue into the darkness. She locked herself in her room as she heard footsteps in the kitchen.

"My Father's come back!" she thought with a sigh of relief, but she first decided to hide the seal from him, putting it into a drawer before going downstairs.

Then she suddenly heard the noise of something being broken. Then silence. Then again more noises, but this time very hasty and nervous sounding, like someone was looking for something they couldn't find. Lunia understood that something strange was happening so she remained silent for a moment, trying to figure out what was going on in the kitchen. Then she panicked when she heard a noisy cough and realised it wasn't her father but someone who had obviously intruded into the house.

"Who was it?" wondered Lunia.

She suddenly thought of the angry man arguing with the blonde woman earlier. Perhaps he had seen Lunia pick up the object? Maybe he had returned to take it back? Maybe soon he would kill her?

Her ghost voices returned "Now you will be punished for what you've done! Bad girl!"

Lunia bravely ignored the voice and decided then to hide herself somewhere safe taking the mysterious object with her, trying not to make any sound. Then suddenly she had the good idea of hiding in the attic which she could reach through a hatch that was built into the ceiling of the bathroom. She should have taken the ladder but it was too risky and there was no time.

Then she took a pole from the closet and with a great swing she reached up to the hook of the lock on the doorway of the hatch. After that the trapdoor opened and she climbed up onto the sink, managing to pull herself up into the attic and close the trapdoor gently behind her.

Unfortunately the intruder was now climbing up the stairs. The sound of his hasty footsteps gave her the impression that he understood where she had hidden herself. There were moments of silence. Lunia heard no noise and for a second she thought the man might have gone but suddenly she heard the bathroom door bang.

"Was he gone or had he just entered?" she wondered to herself in the darkness.

Lunia had no choice but to remain silent and motionless. She stayed still and firm in the darkness of the attic where the light flickered up to her between gaps in the joists below. She was completely paralysed with fear but knew that her lucid mind still had the ability to design a way to salvation.

If the man was still there she would have to escape through a distant roof window. From there she would then have to climb up to reach the balcony and from there climb again, this time down a drainpipe that descended to the ground, and hope that he wouldn't be down there waiting for her.

There was no sound that indicated the presence of this man, so she decided to look down from the attic window to see if he was still there, but she didn't see anyone, only the twisted shadows of the branches of the trees that moved, agitated by the wind, as in a macabre dance.

After several minutes listening she thought that maybe the man was gone. So instead of risking her life unnecessarily by climbing out onto the roof she chose to leave by the stairs. As she walked down she could see that the front door of the house was open. There was only the sound of the wind which was increasing as a thunderstorm came steadily closer.

"The classic 'cherry on the cake'" thought Lunia, smiling finally. "There is no scene of classic terror without lightning and thunder; like something from a film by Dario Argento: maybe I'm a famous actress who has lost her connection with reality?" she rambled to herself nervously "and I'm living on a film set for real life? Oh my God please don't tell me it's that!" she worried, terrified "It would be terrible to lose myself in the fantasy world of celluloid. It would be much better to lose myself in the routine of real life considering how difficult that seems right now."

But destiny prepares strange surprises – even without the intervention of a good director of terror. So Lunia took a big knife from the kitchen just in case she needed it, and she started walking around all the rooms of the house, searching each one in turn. But she didn't see anyone. The man was gone. And finally her parents were coming back!

She could hear the welcome sound of her father's car engine and was finally beginning to relax when she noticed on the kitchen table some traces of the mysterious intruder who had left something for her…

6

ALEX

The Delivery

Two hours after the strange conversation with the unknown man Alex was standing outside in the shadow of the Great Pyramid, when he saw a trail of desert dust behind a van that was obviously heading in his direction.

He got up, exhausted at the prospect of the arrival of yet another visiting official, who would be checking and double-checking his work to make sure that he was being compliant with the agreed archaeological remit. Almost immediately he wanted to somehow send back the vehicle to avoid wasting even more of his precious time on something so mundane and perhaps even absurd that could put him in a situation of ridicule, by delaying his schedule still further. But as the van arrived Alex could see it was more of a delivery van and he became suddenly interested in its presence there.

The man who drove it was a simple youth wearing a long brownish grey tunic typical of the Egyptian style. He had a kind face but moved very slowly, almost as if time for him passed by in another dimension. As Alex observed the youth he found himself revisiting questions he had been fermenting within his mind since his arrival in Egypt.

"What distinguishes us from those people?" thought Alex "What secrets are locked into the awareness of the divine and the mystery which belongs to it? Why did these people radically evolve with such pace and then fall so far into their misery, dropping these people into the shadows of service and charity?"

And yet he knows they are so happy, crowing every working day into physical fatigue with each spiritual chant, a prayer that invokes the faithful to their collective recollections, from one bank to the other of the sacred river that accompanies their beautiful song.

"Good morning mister Tarantino!" said the delivery boy with a smile so strong and sincere that it transformed his gaze with a deeper and fuller energy.

"Good morning to you too! What's your name?" asked Alex

"My name is Mohammed. Nice to meet you. There's a lot of talk about you in town."

"Really? And what interesting things do people say about me?" asked Alex staring into his friendly eyes.

"That the right man from the west has finally arrived and that the secret of the mountain will at last bear its fruit."

"What?" said Alex incredulously "And what does that mean?" he asked in surprise at these clear words from the young Egyptian man.

"The meaning belongs to the history of the men of this Earth. It is not us who can explain the meaning but it is you who must find out by what you are learning, to read between the lines of an ancient language." Then the boy opened the door at the back of the van and handed him a heavy metal box accompanied by an envelope that read:

"Make a treasure of the secrets and make the secrets a treasure."

"What's this?" asked Alex curiously, looking in vain for a clue on the outside of the box.

"I know nothing of the contents Sir" replied the youth "I was merely asked to deliver it to you here." And taking his leave with a slight bow as a sign of respect and reverence, he smiled again, leaving Alex with the box in his hand and the Great Pyramid behind him.

Alex watched the van leave, moving away in its own cloud of dust towards the horizon. And as he did so, he was contemplating that each of the movements of these people seemed to synchronise with the sound of the prayer that was, at that very moment, wafting through the air, like the warm desert breeze that speaks of its ancient lost worlds and their distant roots.

Alex's eyes scanned the horizon whilst, in the distant silence of the desert, a white light blinked momentarily and attracted his gaze and he suddenly noticed that his dry lips were coated with fresh dust – the dust of earth that clouded the environment around him and coated his breath. He took a swig of water from his canteen just as the chant of the desert reached him once more, drifting across the arid landscape to interrupt the silence and join with the whispers of those who have come from afar and are even now, preparing, by unloading armaments, to uncover the secrets of that land, as if it were a box of chocolates that always reserves its many surprises.

Then he took the envelope without a sender and opened it like a child who excitedly opens its gift on its birthday. Inside, a beautifully written note on yellowing card in dark brown lettering that had been styled by hand in henna ink. Its content was very short and concise but it had all the air of a prophecy:

"The key to the door is in your hands, the power of transformation of things, the secret of the Universe. Man has no right to know knowledge – it elevates his soul and then lifts it to Hell."

It was not signed but at the end of the letter on the side was a symbol in the graphology of ancient Egypt which was known as the 'Key of the Afterlife'.

Who could have sent him such a message that was so profound and prophetic but also quite disturbing? Alex had a few moments of self doubt but anxiously reminded himself that this was just part of the mystery that he was entering into and with it came great responsibility. It seemed that he was going to discover something that belonged to his past and now was the time to reconnect with it. For that reason he could not go back or the whole history of humanity would make no sense.

Alex hastened to open the metal box and inside, shielded by handfuls of fresh straw he found a powerful laser cutting tool. He knew that he hadn't ordered it and that it clearly had nothing to do with Bajin as it was an expensive piece of kit. He wondered if it had been sent by the Antiquities department but it was unlikely as there were no other messages inside the box. He took it to his storage area and left it there, for now the most important task was to set up the robotic camera. It was not the simplest of equipment to work with so he knew he would be spending quite a lot of time making it fully operational.

It was nearly sunset by the time the robotic camera finally sprung into life like a small armoured tank that moved easily over any sandy or rocky terrain as if it was going to war to conquer the glory with one last battle which could be full of honours and medals for the courage and sacrifices it made. It was the battle of Alex, the battle of a young American who had dedicated his life so far to his dream: the Discovery of the Mysteries of Ancient Egypt.

The camera was already activated as it moved slowly along the long corridor which would bring it into the room with the gate. The passage was very narrow and dark and Alex could barely see the contours of the walls that were circumscribed by wonderful drawings in well-preserved colours. Each represented scenes of life after death with the accompanying passages, typical of their ancient philosophy with their version of the afterlife.

Each character represented a different God and each God was the symbol of a different planet but what fascinated Alex more was not the strenuous pursuit of life after death, as much as life itself on planet Earth which was completely focused on the spiritual plane above: the almost maniacal dedication to the contemplation of the stars and planets overhead and on which they concentrated so hard to observe a sky so obscure, and so full of mysteries, that even the best modern scientists equipped with the most modern technology have never been able to dismantle it completely.

"Human beings today are no longer able to observe the sky in the same spirit as the Egyptians" thought Alex "and we are not even able to observe the planet on which we live and fully appreciate the wonders that surround us. Today we don't give a damn about life after death and so we also don't give a damn about the future of the planet or its inhabitants, threatened by total destruction and without a way back; a situation which we created."

There had been several hours since the camera had begun transmitting images and now it was finally reaching the exact spot where the opening to the room was supposed to be, when his phone rang.

"Hello? Who is speaking?" asked Alex.

"Congratulations! You have reached the room – well done!" the hoarse male voice commented in the same low tone that had spoken to him previously.

"Who the hell are you?" Alex angrily demanded to hide his increasing concern "I have a right to know if you are trying to control me!"

The voice made a short sarcastic laugh which Alex thought promised nothing good "You are not under my control young man. If you chase yourself through my voice, then you chase your dreams by delegating to me the passages of your destiny. Only you are the maker of these things. You are going along an ancient road of discovery, which is a forgotten memory of a vanished civilisation that left its traces like shards of a shattered temple that has no desire to be rebuilt on this Earth."

"I don't know what you mean and I have no intention of arguing with you as I don't even know who you are! But you certainly do not know what my intentions are on this research!" insisted Alex becoming increasingly alarmed.

"You don't have to explain anything to me about your research" interrupted the voice "I know perfectly well, maybe even better than yourself, what your intentions are, but I can tell you that you are already very fortunate. You have a protection so big that you cannot even imagine. But do not forget that there is a price that you will have to pay for all of this and you will know what that is very soon." And with these words he suddenly ended the conversation leaving Alex speechless in the darkness, realising suddenly that he was in a place very far from home and that idea made him feel uncharacteristically concerned.

The shadows of the evening suddenly seemed like ghosts that he could not escape from, and he felt that this place was clearly the seat of some deep secret which someone felt had to be defended against curious souls like him. Alex settled himself down by telling himself to "focus!" as he watched the images from the robotic camera.

It was finally entering the stone room but the view was a shadowy one and showed nothing obvious, just some slight traces of painting on the walls. Then suddenly the little tank came up against something that prevented it from moving forward. Alex tried to increase the image quality with the various sophisticated filters that were part of the software but still he couldn't see anything.

Then something happened, something extraordinary that is outside of any contact with reality, something that goes beyond any physical or abstract construct; something that left Alex totally without words.

7

LUNIA

The Message

Lunia picked up the paper on which the man had written a message for her and took it up to her room before her parents arrived back home. The letter read:

"Bring back the object you found to its homeland or the curse will strike you and your family for seven generations! You have to go to Hotel Nefertiti in Luxor, Egypt. The object you have is a key that will open a door and you need to find it. Good Luck"

"Luxor? Egypt?" she thought, "but that's impossible! It's too far for me! Or is it?" She suddenly realised that she'd always wanted adventure and this seemed to have come to her, to grant her wishes.

She had never travelled outside of Italy for the fear of flying and not just that, she suffered from agoraphobia which sometimes didn't allow her to leave even her house. She remembered being two or three years old and was playing happily in the field where her grandparents were working when she chased a beautiful butterfly and after a few minutes realised that she was lost and couldn't see her grandparents anywhere. She'd panicked: shouting, screaming and crying.

And since that time grew up without having any sense of directions. If she went, it would be her first adventure. Could the little bird finally leave the nest? It would certainly be a good excuse to leave the house which is something she's wanted to do for a long time. As she heard her parents arguing yet again downstairs she realised that she had to go.

As soon as her parents went to sleep she put a few small things into a backpack and she wrote a letter on the table in exactly the same point where the intruders message had been left for her.

She thought to start the letter compassionately with *"Don't worry...."* But then she realised that they'd never ever been worried for her, so she changed the letter to something more cynical *"I had to go for an training course trip for about one week to Venice and I will call you asap. See you soon - Lunia"* She knew that this would be enough to stop them worrying and she knew they would never start looking for her – they were always too busy arguing.

As she began to pack Lunia reassured her inner voice against the lie that she had written and the guilt it might try to make her feel:

"Venice is not exactly like going to Egypt but it's more believable and everybody goes to Venice once in their life for a honeymoon or as a retirement or romantic trip – even on your own and it would be believed as a popular destination for many educational trips. Venice is par excellence a City that reassures the human soul maybe because of the ubiquitous gondola or the many pigeons in the squares but it is easy to use as an anonymous place to visit." She was to steer her gondola away from Venice to Egypt without anyone else finding out. And the voices were silent.

She put on her trainers, a small jeans jacket and with her bag on one shoulder she headed towards the front door, leaving the house. It was early morning before the Sun begins warming the land and exactly as she had imagined it would be when running away from home. The journey to the train station from the house was a long walk and first she thought to go via the Post Office to take some money out from her savings account that her Grandmother had left for her.

The promise was that she would use the money for when she got married but at that moment Lunia had something much more interesting to do with it than getting married. In her heart she said sorry to her deceased Grandmother as she pressed the buttons on the cash machine with the promise that she would quickly return the money to the account and use it when she was ready to wear the white dress that her Grandmother dreamed of.

She was very keen to take out the little money that was in her Post Office account and that made her feel excited because of the independence it suddenly gave her. Once she got the money she went towards the train station and bought a ticket for Salerno from where she could take the boat to reach Egypt. It was a long trip but cheaper than flying which she was so scared of. She always preferred to feel her feet on the ground even though she was aware that it all depended on destiny. When it is time there is nothing that can save your life, but sometimes for Lunia being rational was not really practical. Her fear started where superstition finished and sometimes we can be a slave to our own fears.

It was still too early to take the train so Lunia decided to go to have a breakfast in the coffee bar by the station. Afterwards she went to the newsagents where outside on the poster board she saw the headlines in large letters which read:

"WOMAN FOUND MURDERED IN REMOTE AREA."

Lunia immediately saw the photograph on the front page which was of the woman she'd seen the day before. She stood in front of the shop quite frozen to the spot and shocked by the news.

The shop keeper asked "Are you okay?" to which Lunia replied:

"Yes I just want a newspaper" and she handed over some small change taking the paper and leaving quickly soon afterwards thinking that this was the beginning of a very difficult time for her.

She was glad to leave the shop because the man was looking at her in a very curious and nosey way and it was obvious that in his usual Tuscan manner he would begin to ask more questions of her. As soon as she was outside the shop she went through the newspaper to read the full story:

"The victim was found dead by a cliff in a rural area, probably after an argument with her killer. The identity of the woman is unknown and she had no personal items that would serve to identify her when she was found apart from a small photograph in her purse which has been reprinted in hope to jolt someone's memory.

The Police have begun investigations stating that it may be a Mafia related crime with the request that no further details are known at this time as identification of the woman was still being ascertained."

Lunia continued to read her description:

"The victim was aged somewhere between 40 and 45, of medium build with blue eyes and blonde hair. Police are hoping to identify her from dental records but if anyone has information about the crime they are encouraged to call in."

Lunia remembered very well how the woman looked and the mysterious object that dropped down from her bag. It was the reason she was now leaving her country and heading for a train to go to Egypt.

She decided that it was probably her duty and a good idea to call the Police, even though she wanted to stay anonymous so that they didn't get in the way of her trip. Also because she wanted to seek revenge for the woman who she believed, probably had an important secret to defend. So she went to a public telephone and called the Police from the kiosk saying:

"I have a few things to say but I will be very clear"

"Who is speaking?" asked the Policeman.

Lunia continued "I can't say who I am but I have to give you some information about the woman who is reported today to have been found dead. I saw her before she was killed. She was arguing with a man with dark skin maybe middle-eastern, probably an Egyptian but I can't say more than that. The woman had with her a little hand bag from which she dropped a strange object deliberately and that object could be the reason why she was killed. I don't think it was a mafia murder – more likely something Political or Religious so good luck with your investigation!" Then she put down the phone without waiting for any reply.

What the consequence of that call would be she didn't care, because she was getting onto the train now and leaving the area. As she sat and relaxed, she was thinking of a beautiful poem she remembered from the book of Veda, a book she liked to refer to when she felt lonely, and she often used it like a good friend to guide her when she felt lost:

"Wind, blow your healthy breezes; blow away Evil. You are the medicine of all this world – the messenger of the Gods"

- Veda RVX, 137,3.

And as the wind blew away the newly fallen leaves the train seemed to fly like the wind, bringing this smiling young woman closer to maturity with each rattle of the tracks. She was just someone who wanted to grow up all too quickly.

8

ALEX

The Picture

In the darkness of a room where no humankind had stepped since about 3000 years before Christ was born, the camera was pointing at something strange which appeared as an image of a faded photograph with a woman who was probably from the early 1900s.

Alex asked himself "How is this possible?" when he saw the image through the camera, projected from a distance of about 500 metres.

The picture was on the floor of the room in which he believed there may be an unidentified tomb, which had never previously been discovered and that nobody knew the existence of. Nobody had been inside before now and all indications were that whoever built the room probably died inside because there was no longer a door and everyone believed that this room was built in order to hold a secret, a sort of security box which was built specifically to allow someone to go in but never to exit.

The long corridor which led to the room was just about wide enough for a human to get through because the ancient Egyptians were believed to have been much smaller than modern humans and it was thought that the tunnel was impossible to travel down. The gate was a real contraption, protected by a lock on the inside with an interlocking mechanism that once hooked up, was impossible to reopen.

The little robot camera was the perfect size to go through the gate and enter the room when suddenly it faced a very strange object, the shape of which was something quite large and it looked like a rock container made from heavy quartz which would hermetically seal anything trapped underneath. It looked like a heavy meteorite that had fallen from above. Maybe everything had been built later around this object? An object that had marked the spot, like a message from God?

Everything could have been accepted if there hadn't been the photograph. How could it be there? Who could it be of? Alex thought that he was dreaming and he hoped to hear the strange voice once again telling him that it was just a joke. What was important was that he would at least have an explanation. But no voice was ready to make him feel more comfortable and he was left feeling abandoned and confused, unable to work out what was going on so he decided to go to the next stage which would involve opening the stone box.

He knew that he now had a laser tool for cutting but first he wanted to very carefully retrieve the photo. The robots tweezers acted as hands to pick up very light things so would be ideal for the photograph. Alex moved the robot very slowly, controlling it remotely. "I need to be really gentle" thought Alex "The picture is very fragile and could disintegrate on contact from the camera." So to avoid losing the image of the face forever he thought it would be a good idea to take a photograph of it, which he did.

It was a face probably between 40-45 years old, with very beautiful lines that were regular and aristocratic. The woman also had very luminous skin which seemed to be almost transparent, bringing light into the dark room, and time hadn't altered this. Her expression was serene and particularly intellectual and unusually portrayed her with both eyes closed in contemplation. It was very difficult to identify any of the original colours because the picture was in sepia but it was evident that she had light brown hair. And what was even more impressive was that she had a beautiful white rose in her hand that she gently posed against her face, like a symbol of innocence. She had a very slight smile on her lips.

It was a perfect picture of a woman from the past and Alex asked himself "To whom was this picture dedicated that was speaking so clearly of love? Her husband? A lover? Or just a dream that was never realised?" It was a mystery but it was certainly a message which had transcended the natural law of time and space to be there after centuries in the very cold interior of the Egyptian tomb; like she had lost her way within the intention of declaring her love.

The little robot went very close to the picture of the beautiful lady with the same delicateness that we usually reserve for taking someone's hand, and by moving its pincers lifted it from the cold pavement and placed it into a metallic box situated behind the engine. The first step was concluded brilliantly so the little robot could return with the prize in its pocket and glory in its heart. It took a little while before the robot returned and Alex was very excited when he watched it coming back through the door from the gallery and instinctively he bent to kiss it as one would a good friend who had returned after a long time of being missing.

Alex quickly cleaned his hands before going to touch the picture and when he saw the picture he was immediately emotional at the sight of such beauty. She was like a pearl of dew in the splendour of the first ray of sunshine that was born above the Great Pyramid.

He took the picture in his hands and gently blew away the dust of the desert which had accumulated on top. Then he turned it over and on the back he saw that there was something written which appeared to be in English: *"The light shines in the darkness and the darkness has not overcome it." – John: Chapter 1: Verse 5.*

It was a phrase from the Gospel which seemed to be like a triumph of life over the things that change, over the time that clears all traces of them, and mostly over the death that transforms them. But what did all these things mean?...

9

LUNIA

Arriving in Egypt

It was dawn when she got off the train. Luxor was different from what she had imagined. It was like a large open yard; half abandoned, half working. The roads were bumpy and full of stones and bricks and almost all the houses nearby were still under construction. She didn't know why nobody was working there. There was an impression that they were waiting for workers to come back after a long break which could be months, years, or maybe they were never coming back.

People were walking on the road with very tranquil steps; mostly men, some women and a lot of children who chased the tourists as they travelled by in their horse and carriages, calling out for 'Bonbons!' and the hopefulness of getting thrown some coins which would make their whole family happy.

Women and men were wearing the same long, plain dress, dark in colour, which for men could vary from light ivory to dark brown but for women was just in black including the scarf which was covering nearly completely their heads, in the Muslim tradition. The smiles and looks they gave were very illuminated and serene which distinguished them as being poor but happy instead of the Europeans who looked rich but depressed.

Very few people could have an easy life here and the few lucky ones seemed to be those who could realise their dream of becoming like Europeans with all the technological advantages of an easier life, without realising that this could be the beginning of their own self-destruction.

Lunia was enchanted to see all these things that made her feel lucky, not only because she was European and could have what was for them just a dream, but also because she could learn about the other side of the coin which hid the secret of happiness.

She was inside her little hotel room when she heard the song that forced her to go to the balcony to watch and listen to the chants that were drifting into the air from all directions, breathing it in until it reached the depths of her heart. It was a message of peace that released endorphins throughout the body. She had just arrived when the waiter from the hotel delivered a message to her, which she silently read:

"Welcome here Miss. I hope the environment is to your liking and that you are ready to conclude our unfinished business, which will cost you not a little effort. You know very well the reason why you are here. The busy-body always has a price to pay! and you, it seems, have decided to pay the expensive price for

curiosity that can put your life at risk, like the gentle lady in Italy who now has her face printed on all the newspapers, but unfortunately as a corpse.

Follow carefully the instructions that you will be given or even you will see your end, with the difference that dying in Egypt is not at all like dying in Italy. Here there is not enough money to waste on photographs for newspapers – or luxury coffins. Here we ignore those facts that waste time, and the right burial for us is to create silence where nobody will disturb us, so try to be a good person if you want to go back to your family safely.

You will soon receive instructions to follow but for the moment, enjoy the view which maybe is not the best but it is the only one we can offer for you. Believe me it could be much worse."

Lunia was puzzled by the sarcastic threats in the letter which had been written on an old typewriter and didn't have a signature on the bottom. Who could be this person who was taking so little care of her and treating her so disgustingly? It was almost certainly the man who a few days earlier had been at her house who could also be the killer of the *'gentle lady'* as he had referred to her.

Lunia sat down on the armchair facing the balcony from which she watched a splendid sunset. It was evening and the air was slightly fresher with a gentle breeze, but even then it was still so hot that she had difficulty breathing. Fatigue prevailed and at last Lunia fell asleep surrounded by a deep silence, broken only by the noise of the river that skirted the hotel garden.

Everything was enveloped in prayer. Everything was in God's hands, a God who had now decided to awaken an ancient power that millennia ago had manifested itself through those original Egyptian citizens, giving them the knowledge of the laws that regulate the Universe and then it was turned off with their disappearance, leaving on this Earth only the traces of their mysteries.

10

ALEX

Faiia's Declaration

After he reprogrammed the robot for the next operation he decided to have a break and he hoped to leave the place very soon. He felt tired and exhausted from the environment that was now becoming sinister and had lost it's fascination for him. It was now manifesting itself in a different light to that which he had previously imagined. The mystery of the Great Pyramid no longer seemed to be part of ancient Egypt but more like a strange and silly joke, disguised as a thriller where the only pleasurable thing seemed to be the beautiful lady of the picture and he wondered if it had been worth risking his career by requesting the camera – maybe just for a picture? But then inside himself he agreed that it was worth it, especially if the beautiful lady could bring him to a new discovery behind the lines of this mysterious enigma.

The robot soon began to march the descending path into the darkness of the tunnel until it had reached that stone safe that dwelt in the middle of the pyramid room, but this time with the right equipment fitted. He knew it wouldn't be easy to open the safe since it was stone but the laser cutter managed to dissect that great rocky mass without damaging it.

When he saw something on the screen that glistened golden yellow and full of promise, he knew it was certainly not trivial. Opening gently the rocky box, he saw in front of his eyes an object that had all the air of being a casket of solid gold! Alex's heart leapt at this sight as it was a typical remnant from a deceased persons personal belongings: something that the ancient Egyptians used to deposit in their tombs along with all the important and expensive artefacts that had belonged to them in life. Unfortunately there was nothing yet that gave any indication as to who these items had belonged to.

The golden casket was sealed and Alex decided to move the robot in a path of 360 degrees to inspect the item before attempting to open it. Then, on the screen, some very strange things appeared. On the top at the left, the box seemed to have signs of damage where it may have been forced previously. There was breakage at the point where the closure met the lid. Someone had already passed by and had awkwardly attempted to open the box leaving a gash of about four centimetres.

Alex decided to send the camera through the slot. The camera was stationed on top of a long arm of the robot which was a flexible tube of one centimetre width. Alex could almost see into the interior of the casket which appeared to be virtually empty, when the camera got stuck against something that was lying in the corner of the box.

Alex used the zoom to focus on a sheet of papyrus which was tightly coiled, and Alex knew that this was going to be his last task for the day, as yet another whim of the Gods. The robot picked up the golden box with the papyrus inside it and returned it to Alex who opened it excitedly and read through the hieroglyphic characters that were written on the papyrus inside.

The message spoke about a precious object that was guarded in the city of Luxor in a sacred place. The manuscript seemed not to be antique but to make sure Alex needed to analyse it in his laboratory. So he decided to conclude his research and step back from this scenario where everything was taking on the air of a personal drama without any logical connection, and where the director and the writer had abandoned the story to itself.

At that moment Alex's phone rang. He couldn't believe that the man with the hoarse voice was going to make contact with him at such an important instant but as he answered the call he was greeted by the sound of Mister Bajin's voice.

"I've made a real breakthrough!" blurted Alex, unable to contain his excitement.

"What is it?" replied Bajin swiftly.

"A golden casket – it was inside the rock box that I managed to open without damaging - thanks to the robot!" explained Alex.

"That's wonderful news indeed! Bring it here to my office at once" Bajin ordered "and bring the robot too" he added forcefully.

"What?" exclaimed Alex "But I can't proceed without the robot! What are you telling me?"

"Exactly that" replied Bajin "The Government has told us it's use has been withdrawn, so we are no longer authorised to have it."

"From when exactly?" said Alex unable to believe what he was hearing.

"From exactly now!" Bajin yelled "I just got off the phone speaking to them. Bring it back Alex! This excavation project is over - for now."

Alex ended the call feeling more frustrated than ever before. "How can the project be finished when I made such an important discovery? And how can I ignore the message I found on the papyrus?" He knew he had to make possibly the most important decision of his life and he had to make it now.

Alex found himself involved in having to take back the reins of a masterpiece abandoned by someone who perhaps had been afraid. He went back to Mister

Bajin's office feeling furious, as he handed back the robot with its tools that he had used.

"Take back whatever you wish" said Alex angrily, fully aware that this was going to be the last time that they would be meeting, posting on his desk the list of robotic tools alongside the golden box.

Bajin leaned forward and took possession of the box with a broad smile on his face.

"Nothing makes you more happy than money does it? Nothing can satiate your hunger for gold! I just want to say I'm leaving and so this is 'Goodbye'!" and with that Alex left and slammed the door behind him, not allowing Mister Bajin the chance to reply.

Faiia the secretary was waiting in the room next door when she saw Alex and understood that he was intending to leave for good.

She stopped him and said "Wait don't go! Not without taking me with you."

Alex was surprised by her words and didn't know how to respond but she carried on speaking "You believe that you will discover an important archaeological find but instead you've found me. I'm the reason you are here. You were looking for something dead but instead you've found something living. I am still very much alive and I can still change the road and my destiny, with your help. Let's climb together the mountain of success, and kiss me when we arrive there, because I have something to conquer, me too, I can love someone and it's you."

At these words Alex was knocked backwards in disbelief. He didn't understand if the young woman was talking like that because she was delirious or because she had been there for such a long time, watching him visit each day, that she had fallen in love with him, and now she couldn't hide it any more; like the explosion that lightening makes when it hits the side of an oak tree and exposes its inner fibres.

For the first time Alex saw Faiia in a different light and he had the impression that she had been dreaming all this time, a dream of a very selfish and childish love which was pathological but unfortunately very common to a lot of people who have obviously failed in previous relationships. Alex then felt a deep compassion towards her, because she was so little and yet her passion was so big, and she was obviously expressing a deep love that she had dreamed for so long.

"You have a vision of life that is very consumeristic" said Alex as he looked sweetly into her eyes "Life is not something that can be bought and sold: it passes quietly between things and is consumed in its own flow, between the vibrations of the cosmos to be reborn with the intention of creating, and not to destroy as you do by your need for possession." And with these words Alex left her with a kindly smile.

Faiia was a very beautiful young woman with dark eyes and olive skin, sweet and generous enough to make any man grateful but that was not the right moment for him. She was probably the right woman at the wrong moment. Alex walked out through the door and left her in the same office that they had met in, so long ago. He didn't forget her easily and from time to time she came into his mind, especially during the loneliest nights.

She would never see him again but that encounter was imprinted on her mind as some deep wisdom that she would benefit from in the future and it changed her life forever. Faiia would never fall in love with another man for many years, but she gained a deep sense of serenity within herself which allowed her to have a rich emotional life, devoting herself to voluntary work caring for abandoned children.

And it was when she thought to retreat into solitude that she found love. He was a doctor who was working within a religious community with the purpose of helping orphaned children and together they joined their experiences along the same path, united by a profound feeling that went beyond the love of a couple, but the love of life that they together gave to others.

11

LUNIA

The Second Message

The following morning Lunia received another message. Very short and straight to the point:

"Meet me at 12.30pm by the Karnak Temple and bring with you the object that you must deliver. A man with a black tunic and a briefcase will meet you for the delivery."

Lunia felt quite frustrated thinking about giving the precious object to someone she didn't know before she had discovered its true meaning. She didn't like the idea of being there and risking her life, only to be a delivery girl of something so important. The fact that she had to be blackmailed and used in this way for some reason made her think about a way she could change the direction of this situation by following her instinct. She wanted to make it clear by interrupting her communication with the mystery man, and thought about abandoning her hotel immediately, only she didn't know where to go.

12

ALEX

Moving to Luxor

Mister Bajin was just the first step in a long line of adventures. Alex knew that this man was a crook but he didn't know who the other people were who were involved in this dirty business, probably the same people who would soon be waiting for him at Luxor where he had decided to head, following the indication on the papyrus he had found in the Great Pyramid.

Alex moved into the city of Luxor where a friend invited him to live with him, for a break from the stress of his work. During the trip he had time for long reflections on his adventures there so far and he began to feel disillusioned with his principle idea of becoming an archaeologist. He loved his job but he felt like abandoning it, because of the corruption that seemed so entwined in it. As he allowed himself to be gently rocked to sleep by the train he hoped that he would be given some answers in his dreams.

When he arrived at his destination he began looking for somewhere to have breakfast. As he walked between the crowds of people moving on the street he saw something ahead that caught his attention and he stopped to focus on what was going on.

13

LUNIA

The Escape

She was running fast between people, holding on tight to a small bag that she was protecting against the rest of the world like a vulnerable child. She looked tired even though her youth was giving her plenty of energy to move fast from a predator.

Behind her a man was running fast, he looked dangerous in elegant dress and dark sunglasses that hid his face which appeared from its lines like middle-eastern, maybe Egyptian. The young woman looked European and as Alex focused on her, he realised that she might be in danger and decided that he must get to her, to try to help.

He ran towards her and hid by the corner an unfinished building so he could observe when the woman was going to be passing. When finally he heard her rapid footsteps and panting, he jumped out, grabbing her suddenly by the arm and covered her mouth with his other hand to prevent her from screaming. He dragged her into a doorway, staring her straight in the eyes to let her know somehow that he was there to help and reassure her.

The woman appeared very scared and at the same time he had the feeling that he knew her, like she was the face of someone from his past and this was another piece of the puzzle. He couldn't yet understand the connections in this story where the protagonists seemed like improvising actors, borrowing their parts from pieces of lives spread all over the place but about to reconstruct themselves into some new story guided by a strange mystery.

14

ALEX & LUNIA

The Meeting

The man who was following Lunia lost track of her and after stopping for a few moments to look around him, ended up going off in the wrong direction. When Lunia was quiet, Alex asked her the reason she was there and what was happening. Lunia seemed too innocent to be involved in any dark organisation and she didn't look like a professional or someone who was working under the control of any gangs, so who could she be, this particular pearl – lost in the middle of the desert sand?

When Lunia had time to calm down and began to trust her instincts once more, she looked into Alex's eyes and felt that he was someone she could trust. So she decided to explain herself to him "I travelled alone after I got this letter which told me where I had to go." She showed Alex the letter.

"And who gave you this letter?" asked Alex, not totally believing her story at this point.

"It was a man who came into my house in Italy after he saw me at the scene of a crime." she explained innocently.

"Crime?" said Alex very surprised and somewhat shocked "Then this story has started to be really serious" and he suggested to Lunia that they should leave the area and go to somewhere more safe where no-one could find her. Alex then called his friend Jabril explaining in a few words that he needed to bring Lunia along with him and Jabril agreed to receive his friend.

Jabril was an Egyptian who came from a wealthy family. He studied archaeology in Cairo and met Alex during an excavation job they had together by the Valley of the Queens and the Kings, and where they became good friends.

He always sustained the theory that says "For each discovery there would be a message from the Gods so it shouldn't be done with the purpose of profit but to enrich the culture" and for that reason each discovery he made was followed by a ritual of prayers and giving thanks, as the meaning of each piece was found and made public, as proof of being a message from the Gods.

When Jabril opened the door of his house he was very pleased to see his good friend Alex but he was wondering who this woman was with him and what her story was.

"So tell me what brings you here?" he asked Lunia as he finished setting up some tea for his guests.

Alex interrupted him saying "She is just someone who is involved in a mysterious story which brought both of us us here and she needs help. It's not a coincidence that we met but I still have to understand what the connection is. My life is starting to feel like a dream from which I wish to wake up." Alex was very tired and didn't like not being in control of the situation, and yet he found himself again involved in a strange story against his will. Suddenly his life it seems will follow another destiny: "The Destiny of Gods".

Alex asked Lunia to tell them both her story and in particular the details in order to try to find why they had met in Egypt. So Lunia spoke about the woman she saw by the window and the man who attacked her and forced her to go in his car, then she showed the object that dropped out of the woman's bag and explained that it was the reason why she had come to Egypt.

Alex couldn't believe his eyes when he saw the object which was shaped as an 'Ankh', an ancient Egyptian hieroglyphic symbol that was most commonly used in writing and in art to represent the word for "life" and, by extension, as a symbol of life itself. According to the ancient scriptures it was the key of the Gods – the key to gaining access to the afterlife in the eternal spiritual dimension,and it seemed to come from the Great Pyramid where he had been working until a few days before the only difference being that his picture was from the beginning of the 19th Century.

Lunia showed the picture of the woman in the newspaper who had been killed. When Alex saw that face he thought he'd gone crazy. Then he took out from his briefcase the picture of the mysterious lady that he had recovered from the Great Pyramid and he put it next to the newspaper image. She seemed so similar with

"Suddenly some pieces of this puzzle are beginning to take shape" thought Alex and then he took out the papyrus that he'd found in the Great Pyramid and kept for himself.

On the papyrus there was a message written in hieroglyphics which read:

"Seek the precious object hidden in a sacred place in Luxor city"

and then underneath there was a drawing of an Ankh. It was the same shaped symbol as the object that Lunia found.

Her Ankh was particularly luminescent and sculptured in gold characters and adorned with precious stones. It was a about the size of a small pen and it looked like it might contain something inside. Alex observed the object very closely trying to understand its meaning and it was clear that the papyrus and the object belonged to the same tomb and held the same secret that was hiding behind that door of the sacred place in Luxor.

As Alex moved the object in his hand he felt that one of the stones seemed slightly lose and as he touched it and looked more closely it began to turn 180 degrees and the top began to open so that he could see inside a small metal tube.

Suddenly their faces became full of amazement as they noticed the little tube had, written around it, numerous ancient symbols. Alex wondered if it might be another clue with which they could reach the sacred place, however the writing was symbolic and still needed to be translated. The ancient message was formulated for just a few people to understand, the ones that knew the 'Language of Gods'.

It was then that Alex received a new call from the mysterious man with the croaky voice "You believed that you could abandon this case so easily but you didn't consider that it was the case that didn't abandon you."

Alex knew that he must be on the right track. It had been several days since this man had been in touch but his timing was so perfect that Alex felt he must be observing them somehow, ready to give him more instruction.

"So you are still alive?" said Alex, surprised to hear again the man with no face and no name "Who are you?" asked Alex "and why do you insist in keeping in the shadows without having the courage to show yourself?"

"That is exactly what I was going to tell you." said the voice "My name is Hammed."

"And what do you want from me Hammed? If you want something specific speak clearly now and don't waste my time!" insisted Alex.

"I have something to show you which you will find very interesting" Hammed continued "and which will help you to understand this strange story. Everything is written down in a diary that has been stolen and you should try to find it – it's very important."

"So you're telling me that I should steal a diary from somebody I don't know Mister Hammed? Are you mad?" Alex summarised incredulously.

"I'm telling you that if you want light on the story, to see why you are involved, you need to proceed as I suggest, or everything you've done up to know will be worth nothing" Hammed explained.

"Right let's get to the point – where is that diary?" asked Alex impatiently.

"The diary is in the hands of a very dangerous person who, in this story, represents the real enemy from whom you need to defend yourself. So I think now is the best time to meet up face to face if we want to co-operate in this situation."

"Good idea!" said Alex "Finally I am going to have a face to this voice which has persecuted me for quite a while now. Tell me where and when you want to meet up."

"Now" said Hammed determinedly "at 5.30pm at Karnak Temple"

"So in about one hour" confirmed Alex glancing at his watch, feeling a shivering down his back with excitement and preparing himself for the moment he would meet this man at last.

"But Karnak Temple is exactly the place I was told to meet when I decided to change the plan and you found me as I was being chased" recounted Lunia in a very concerned way "Do you think it's a trap?"

Alex thought about the situation carefully but decided to go alone leaving Lunia with Jabril assuring her that she was in good hands and that he would be returning as soon as possible.

When he arrived at the temple he was looking for Hammed between the few people who were walking around the area of the sacred ruins that after millennia were still so well preserved. All of their majesty was still evident in the columns which were sculptured with figures of Egyptian Pharaohs who once ruled the city.

Alex was looking around for Hammed but was lost from time to time in the beauty and mystery of this structures that had belonged to such extraordinary people to which he felt very deeply devoted.

He felt that he was there to bring light to an enigma belonging to other people living long before him, then abandoned to the events of destiny, just waiting to be rediscovered again. It was in the same instant that he was mesmerised by the beauty of the scenery that he noticed a man coming towards him in dark dress and dark sunglasses, sitting in a wheelchair.

When he was closer Alex could see on his face very evident scars that ran from one side of his head to the other and gave him an even harder appearance than he had imagined. He was a man who was very secure and confident despite being in a wheelchair and it was evident that he didn't readily accept his disabled state by the way that he moved his big body quite neurotically. Alex guessed that he was a proud man who didn't readily accept his situation.

"Welcome Hammed" said Alex gently.

"You are welcome too Alex" said Hammed in the distinctively hoarse voice that Alex immediately recognised from their phone calls together. "You are very young and I'm not surprised that user Bajin lost you. He takes advantage of young researchers and treats them like excavators" he said sarcastically with a sense of revenge and bitterness.

"That is the reason why I left that place. But how do you know Mister Bajin?" asked Alex in surprise.

"It's a long story, but it's one that I am going to tell you now, because we have something in common, me and you. A long time ago I was in partnership with Mister Bajin and for many years we worked together without any problems, in fact we had a lot of success in the field of Archaeology and we trusted each other, with our business operations giving sustenance to more than a thousand workers. Everything was proceeding well, until the day I met someone who gave me a diary.

That person was a man who didn't speak much, but he knew something very big and important which could upset the World. He told me that he was dying and he wished to go on one last mission and that he needed my help, but I should keep it a secret and not tell anyone, especially mister Bajin my business partner at that time.

This man gave me the diary which was written in beautiful handwriting, yellowed from time, but otherwise well maintained. At first I thought it was a joke, but the man recommended that I read it carefully because it mentioned an ancient secret which revealed how to find a seal - the key to open a door.

The space behind it contained something, a kind of Holy Grail: an instrument that held an important secret in the Story of Humanity, which was formulated by the Egyptian civilisation at its conclusion. It is the concentration of thousands of years of research that is contained within this mysterious object, and it has been hidden in a secret place all this time.

The diary was written by a female archaeologist named Elizabeth Darren who lived around the 1920s. She belonged to an esoteric congregation founded by one of her ancestors in 1800 in Edinburgh, where she was born. The congregation was meant to safeguard the great secret which was mentioned in the diary. She found a mysterious invaluable object during one of her archaeological excavations by the Great Pyramid.

Elizabeth wrote down all her discoveries in this diary, where she reported even the details of magic formulas and manuscripts that were part of the heritage and culture of that congregation, and it is in that diary that I could read the most hidden secret. That brought me to discover the narrow hidden passage, where I was found nearby nearly dead after a landslide. At the time I was trying to go through the door with the gate."

"But from what you are telling me Hammed" interrupted Alex "it seems that there was something more than a landslide".

Hammed continued to explain how he was struck on the back from someone who stole the diary and the Seal.

Alex knew that this was probably the same Seal that years later had been found by Lunia, after she saw it dropped by a woman who was later killed in Italy.

"So was it you who made an appointment to meet up here today with Lunia?" Alex demanded.

"Certainly not but this means that somebody else is looking for the Seal." Hammed responded.

"What strange disparate connections with facts so apparently separated, which have now drawn us all together in Luxor!" thought Alex not fully satisfied enough to believe Hammed yet.

Alex was listening in silence as he looked at that experience-hardened face. The man told his story whilst turning occasionally on the chair that had been transporting him for some time; since the day he was hit twice in the Great Pyramid, first by the man who then robbed him, and then from the "Fury of the Gods" as they used to say in those parts of Egypt; they punished hard anyone attempting to profane their sacred places which was exactly what had happened to Hammed, and according to such beliefs he was now forced to travel in this wheelchair.

Alex didn't know any more if what this man was telling him was the truth. He was profoundly troubled and confused but he knew he had to go on trying to clarify his understanding.

"So the Seal was still in the pyramid even though it was already discovered by Elizabeth?" exclaimed Alex "If so, what did Elizabeth find that was so important, during her original excavations?"

"Elizabeth had discovered the secret passage which led to the Seal, better known as an Ankh or key, whatever you want to call it, since it's function is to open the door." Hammed continued "Unfortunately in 1920 there were no appropriate means to access such dark and small tunnels and using dynamite was too dangerous. That's why Elizabeth guarded the secret of her discovery, inside her diary. But she had never been able to withdraw the Seal from the room of the Great Pyramid."

"How did she know about the Seal then?" asked Alex.

"That is exactly what I was going to tell you. The day she was involved in excavations near the Great Pyramid it is reported that she fell into a deep trance state for many hours and nobody from the team could awaken her. After she awoke she recorded this in her diary, it's what happened to her during the trance:

"I fell into the darkest state of my mind when a light came towards me from far away and when it got closer to me I realised it was a being, with a very beautiful female face, who revealed her identity as Queen Nefertiti. She gently held my hand, inviting me to follow her inside the Great Pyramid where we crossed narrow passages without any effort or difficulty even though I knew it was impossible for any human being to go through.

It was at that moment that I realised we were both in spirit form. When we arrived in front of a gate of a secret room which was empty apart from a large rock container in the middle. Inside the rock container was another golden box which held a Seal called an Ankh. She told me that this object was the key to open the door to a sacred place in Luxor. Nefertiti encouraged me to record this information as now was not the right time to obtain the Seal but through my writings somebody else could access it in the future."

"When I was given the diary and read this account I decided to follow her instructions to recover the Seal. I realised it would be difficult to gain access to the passages so I arranged through Bajin to hire the same robot that you later used for your excavations."

"That explains why I had such resistance from Bajin to hire it for my work" said Alex "he obviously wanted to hide from me the previous problems he'd had with you. So you were there before me! And now perhaps you can tell me the secret of how you seemed to know exactly what I was doing while I was in the Great Pyramid?"

"When I was rescued, and the robot was returned to Bajin, nobody realised that there was a second remote viewing unit that was still in my pocket after the 'accident' and it allowed me to see everything that you were seeing, so I was able to call you at each discovery" smiled Hammed looking pleased with himself. "The operation would have been perfect if I hadn't been discovered by mister Bajin and he had me followed by one of his henchmen to have me killed so he could keep the Seal for himself.

Fortunately, I'm still alive, but only because just after the man hit me in the back, a landslide happened that could have ended up killing me, but instead it saved my life because the man was forced to flee and abandon the area, or he would have remained trapped there with me. But before he left, he took both the diary and the Seal from me, and he never delivered it to mister Bajin."

"He never delivered it? But I thought you said he worked for Bajin?" queried Alex.

"I only knew afterwards, when I found out that this man who previously was working for Bajin had been paid a lot of money to betray him."

"By who?" Alex interrupted.

"By exponents of the Esoteric Congregation which Elizabeth was part of. But now the rest of the story is up to you and your female friend who, for some reason, came into possession of the Seal."

Alex understood that Hammed would have to join him if he wanted to piece together the rest of this puzzle. Moreover they would not be able to carry on this discovery if they didn't work together. They needed each other, and so for that reason Alex invited Hammed to follow him to his current home, where Jabril and Lunia were waiting for him. The first thing Alex decided to do for Hammed was to show him the picture of the beautiful lady found in the Great Pyramid. Hammed immediately recognised Elizabeth's face in the picture.

"I remember seeing that photograph via the robot camera when you found it. It belonged to the diary that was stolen from me, and that day it must have detached from the page and fallen to the ground without anyone noticing it until you found it during his excavations Alex. But that wouldn't explain how it came to be so far down the tunnel." commented Hammed.

"It's possible the landslide could have created a wind flow down the tunnel that would be strong enough to carry a small photograph" suggested Alex.

"Actually I had a real sensation of being drawn into the narrow tunnel while I was there" Hammed confirmed "I wondered if it could have been Nefertiti's spirit influencing things once more?"

Then Alex showed Hammed the papyrus "This was found inside a golden box. It says *'Seek the precious object hidden in a sacred place in Luxor city'.*"

"Well" said Hammed "I see with joy that you have carried on a task that I started but never finished. I broke the box while retrieving the Seal with the robot but didn't get time to collect the papyrus. But there's still something missing: maybe the most important piece – the Seal to open the secret door."

It was at that point that Lunia stepped forward, and showed him the precious object that she had found in the grounds of her family house.

Hammed took the Ankh tenderly in his hands "Well! We meet again!" he spoke to the Seal and returning to Lunia he added "How did you find it?"

She explained how she came into possession of the beautiful object that she saw falling from the handbag of the woman who was later found dead: killed in the Tuscan countryside.

"So many people seem to die when they come into contact with this beautiful object" Hammed commented, peering down mournfully at the wheelchair that carried him and adding sadly "I wonder how many more people have to die?"

Alex and Lunia were also concerned and felt the fear of death that seemed to follow this mystery with its apparent curse. They both wished it would come to its final conclusion safely but knew they had a long way to go yet.

Then Lunia took from her backpack the Italian newspaper article and told Hammed about the murdered woman, leaving him surprised and with baited breath, as Alex had felt before. Hammed recognised that the woman who had been killed had the same face as the woman on the picture that Alex had found in the Great Pyramid: the archaeologist Elizabeth.

"Two women that looked impressively similar, linked by the same story, but living in two different time eras: the mystery was becoming more and more intriguing" thought Hammed.

"Inside the Ankh was a small metal tube and it looks to me like these hieroglyphic signs could be a clue of the secret place?" Alex suggested showing Hammed the tube.

Hammed leant forward and smiled as he cast his eyes over the symbols "This is written in an ancient language known as the 'Language of the Gods'. I have studied it for years so will be the best person to decode it for you, but it will not be easy and could take several days at least."

"Well now I'm wondering who that woman was, and why was she in possession of the Seal? And why did she then throw it from her bag before the man could get it?" pondered Alex.

At this point they had to try to discover the identity of the woman who was killed in the Tuscan countryside.

"We have to go to Italy" said Alex "Police investigators can tell us the identity of this woman and why she was murdered. I'll call them to tell them we'll be coming over so they can prepare the information we need."

"You should go with Lunia" commented Hammed with a frustrated air because he was the only one who couldn't move as he wished, due to that damned wheelchair. "She's also Italian, and she can guide you to the right people you will need to address. In the meantime I will be working on translating the symbols on the mystery tube."

"I'm happy to return to the land of my birth" Alex said, giving Lunia a knowing smile "and it'll be good to practice my Italian again!"

15

ALEX & LUNIA

Italy

For Lunia it was a good reason to return home as her excuse of being on a tour in Venice wouldn't hold for much longer, and she had called her parents very few times since she had departed for Egypt. She didn't miss them and she wished to travel around the world much more for new adventures, but she was aware that she needed to complete her studies at college and, without finances of her own, she could not decide her life for herself yet, even though she realised that she had always been alone and that her freedom would end up where she started: with the fear of being alone, and without anyone telling her the limits that she could have to her life, she felt abandoned.

Alex didn't want to interfere with her private life but he was observing her when she wasn't looking and he noticed that in her long silences, her gaze was lost in emptiness. She had the mixed air of a lost child but sometimes of a woman aware of her own existence, and of her will to affirm her existence in a changing world that is like a crazed horse: hard to ride if you don't have the reins firmly in your hand.

Once they arrived in Italy Lunia went home and Alex booked into a hotel in the area after Lunia warned him that he wouldn't be comfortable staying in her house within the chaos of her parents constantly arguing. In the following days Alex became a familiar face, with visits Lunia's home to meet her family, and most importantly, to see the area where the kidnapping took place.

"And here is where it happened" said Lunia indicating to the area during the time that they were slowly walking in the fields surrounding the house. Alex's concentration was lost in his fascination with the Tuscan countryside; its colourful hues made it so romantic, and the smell of the newly cultivated land triggered memories of a past lived in some remote place in that ancient land, full of endless passion.

Alex went back in time as he walked the vineyards and saw himself again as a child. He was the son of an Italian mother and an American father who lived in Italy during the first years of his life. When his father decided to move to America with the whole family for economic reasons it was the years of the economic boom, and many people made their fortunes in foreign countries. Many Italians moved to America, and his father who lived in Italy for many years, felt the need to go back to his homeland, where he was expecting a better future.

Alex had always wanted to return to Italy one day, to discover his roots on that wonderful land, which by coincidence and destiny had called him back again, giving him the feeling of never having left. He took steps measured by time itself as he retraced his past, slowly through the green mantle of new growth with shades of light brown earth: conscious steps that came back to life as never before, and he could see himself as a small boy walking on fresh grass looking for insects to observe and then running to hunt butterflies, until the voice of his mother recalling him from the window, brought him home for dinner.

"Alex, Alex!" It was Lunia who shouted to him as he was busy within his own world, kidnapped for a moment in a haze of memories and absent to reality and she saw him slipping away serenely, forgetting for a while the reason why he was over there.

"Alex, is everything all right?" she said to him, taking him by the arm.

"Yes, sorry I lost myself in the incredible beauty of nature, for a moment" replied Alex abruptly returning to reality "We have to go to the Police and tell them the facts. Maybe they have already established the identity of the woman?" wondered Alex.

And so they found themselves in the Police Chief's office who had conducted the investigation and had reopened the file that contained the photos of Sarah Shiff which appeared to be the name of the woman who had been killed, and she was even an archaeologist and of Scottish descent – just like Elizabeth.

She was in Italy for work, but they hadn't yet managed to establish who Sarah had come into contact with before she died. Alex showed the photo he already had of Elizabeth to the Officer, who was left in no doubt that she closely resembled Sarah.

After a careful observation of the two photos the Officer concluded "But this looks like it is the same woman in two different eras! We have to investigate whether these woman are linked in some way by parentage."

"Or maybe something else?" added Alex.

16

THE TWO WOMEN

The Esoteric Egyptian Society

Police investigations had so far brought to light that Sarah Shiff was the great grand-daughter of Elizabeth and both were archaeologists forming part of an esoteric group founded by Elizabeth herself in 1920. The Police had become interested in the group originally as a potential terrorist organisation, but later dropped their enquiries as their suspicions had proved groundless. Much of the information they had on file was historical and Alex and Lunia sifted through it looking for clues that would help them resolve their own mystery.

Sarah had become a priestess of the same congregation in 2000. The group was founded on Elizabeth's discoveries on esoteric studies in ancient Egypt. The majority of the congregational attendants were from the worlds of archaeology, anthropology, psychology and literati of the same nature, all orientated in discovering what is hidden behind the archetypal symbolism of an ancient civilisation like Egypt.

The final reality they protected with extreme security, both materialistically by extremely safe constructions like the pyramids, and esoterically by mystifying the energy behind false appearances, to safeguard them from the malignant forces of those who would use such knowledge to profit from; for the purpose of trying to control entire humanity. They had already understood thousands of years ago, that economic power was only a façade that concealed an even more dangerous movement in the hands of those few who held the power of control, for purely material purposes.

The documentation showed that Elizabeth had devoted herself to such research and was the founder of the 'Esoteric Egyptian Society' and Sarah, the great-granddaughter of Elizabeth years later became their new leader, taking the title of priestess and introducing into the group a new doctrine aimed at expanding esoteric knowledge not only from a cultural, but also from a spiritual point of view, thus transforming the title to the 'Esoteric Egyptian Spiritual Society.'

This gave rise to the doctrine of a spiritual order where the group members became true disciples, ready to take priestly orders that Sarah had made available to them (with the introduction of the Franciscan Fathers Union Acts) to a new order of pagan origin.

"It appears that Sarah had created a new esoteric order and therefore a new religion" remarked Alex.

"And the whole concept became masterfully directed by Sarah" added Lunia, "with the aim of making known the 'Ultimate Reality' through religious filters."

Alex found himself wondering "what was this 'Ultimate Reality' that was so fanatically protected and jealously guarded within the meandering maze of secret tunnels and seals, for which people like Sarah and Elizabeth had risked their lives?"

Lunia too was wrapped in her own troubling queries "Why, at the end of this story, did everything come back to a Seal in a door?" she thought "and what was actually behind that door? (if it really existed)."

These and many others, were the questions that were in the minds of Alex, Lunia and the Police Chief at that time.

In his miserable life and career the Police Chief had arrested no more than ten people, for the usual boring problems of a society that sees nothing but drug trafficking, bribes and prostitution. Always the same diet for years without variations on the horizon, when finally he got the cherry on the cake: something different which had made the antennas of the poor officer prick up. He felt for the first time alive and full of energy, ready to dig into deeper investigations of a sensational case that went beyond all limits. It was something that finally made him feel more important than ever.

"From our investigation it has emerged that Sarah was travelling often between Italy, Egypt and Scotland so some secret mission linked these countries" reported the Police Chief giving a big twist to his investigative problems, but making him feel like Sherlock Holmes.

Alex checked the internet for more information. The "Esoteric Egyptian Spiritual Society" had more than 100,000 adepts spread all over the world. It was based in Edinburgh where it was founded but spread like wild fire to all those countries where the priests had been indoctrinated to the disclosure of its essence:

"God is the energy light that by nature belongs to us and that we can manage with thought by directing it to wherever we want and get the benefits that we need" read Alex on the website introduction,

"It's like a Divine Alchemy which described the congregation through socio-cultural and spiritual notions that were rather interesting" he continued:

"And as in ancient Egypt we are able to manipulate this energy only through our awareness of the 'Ultimate Reality' that we have unfortunately been denied for thousands of centuries, by those who wanted to transform a free and divine society, into a society enslaved by profit and matter, better known as money."

The content was very interesting and it made him think that Elizabeth and Sarah were two pearls in a long, precious chain which stretched to the ends of the world, propagating an ancient melody that reached into the infinite space of the Universe.

Alex took this information with the feeling that the content had some deeper meaning for him as well, and had belonged to him for ever; he felt that he was finally achieving a deeper meaning that he had been searching for since his first interest in archaeology.

Then he searched through the names of the Italian adepts so he could visit them while he was in Italy and investigate more directly. One of them was that of the Brother Gino known as friar Sun whose on-line profile elaborated:

"the one who rises early in the morning with the sunrise and retires with the sunset, dedicating his prayers and his alchemic functions during the daylight hours, as the symbology of the inner light better known as the divine light".

"He lives in Perugia at a small Franciscan community in the middle of a forest which is difficult to get to, or even find a beaten path: the ideal place for those who do not want to be distracted by the surrounding noisy world. Perfect for anyone wishing to remain undisturbed" declared Alex.

Alex decided to visit Friar Sun, while the Police Chief directed his investigations more on Elizabeth's past by trying to uncover the roots of that mysterious alchemical world, that over the years had spread in the wise silence of those who knew the 'Ultimate Reality'. Lunia wanted to go to the monastery with Alex but unfortunately women were not allowed to enter, so she returned home to await news from him.

17

FRIAR SUN

The Alchemy of the Spirit

When Alex arrived at the front of the small Franciscan monastery, he had the feeling of being in a world of fables that time had not touched. The peace and serenity of that place was the real milestone that man always seeks in the most diverse places of the world, without knowing that there are certain remote communities so small that they are camouflaged in their simplicity, but they are also great in their divine manifestation; which emanates with the morning light to the confines of the Universe, to retire again in the evening when the Sun goes to sleep.

When Alex found himself in front of the door of that ancient structure that stood so majestically on the top of the hill, he felt so at peace with himself that he almost forgot the reason he had come there.

The man who came to open the door to him was a friar with a kind appearance and a quiet gaze, worthy of a man who dedicates his life to the humble prayer of thanksgiving, for the beauty of nature that surrounds him.

"I'm looking for Brother Gino or friar Sun" Alex said in a subdued tone.

"He will be here in a second" replied the little friar, almost as if he had been waiting for him.

After a few minutes Friar Sun appeared from the back of the room where Alex was waiting. He was around forty, aristocratic looking but at the same time very humble with a sociable and approachable nature.

"Tell me, mister...?" said the friar as he arrived behind Alex.

"Alex Tarantino. Pleased to meet you Brother Gino" answered Alex, holding out his hand in greeting.

"You can call me friar Sun – it's the name by which I am known, since I recognised in myself the alchemical power of the divine light that we visualise as sunlight."

"I understand. " said Alex with a moment of perplexity.

"How can I help you mister Tarantino?"

"I'm here to ask you to identify a person's face" and so saying he pulled out the newspaper page on which Sarah's photo was printed.

The friar looked at the piece of newspaper as if he'd seen an apparition of Our Lady. He moved away from the page and looked down to try to prevent Alex noticing the tears that fell from his eyes.

"I'm sorry to recall such bad memories" said Alex feeling rather embarrassed.

"Never mind, I knew someone would come here sooner or later looking for her. She already knew, before she died that someone one day would knock on this door to do justice for her untimely death that she had already prepared herself for. Sarah was endowed with psychic sensibilities and could see into the future, so she wrote down what happened to her."

After these words, the man invited Alex to follow him into the adjoining room, where he made him sit down on a soft couch in front of a warm burning fire place. Then once he sat down and relaxed the friar continued to speak of Sarah.

"Sarah was the daughter of a couple from Scotland who were all part of the Esoteric Community. She was born and raised in the same environment that also saw her die. She had become one of the highest exponents of the Congregation itself. She was a woman with a revolutionary spirit, and she demonstrated it by bringing new theories and new mystical practices.

"And what about this other woman?" asked Alex showing the picture of Elizabeth.

"Elizabeth!" said the friar with a startled air "She was an ancestor of Sarah. She was the founder of the Congregation. But where did you find this picture?"

"I found it myself in Egypt while I was digging in the Great Pyramid" said Alex

"So you are also an Archaeologist!?" said the surprised friar.

"Yes" confirmed Alex "and the reason I'm here, and why I found this picture, is because I have become involved a series of coincidences that have led me to investigate the disappearance of Sarah which seems somehow to be connected to the discovery of a mysterious object by a young woman named Lunia. She saw Sarah's abduction when Sarah voluntarily dropped the object from her purse before being kidnapped, and was made to climb into the vehicle of her executioner."

Friar Sun was shocked by those words, and did not know where to begin to make sense of the events that had brought this young man Alex to the front door of his monastery, but he knew that both of them were linked within the same destiny, and that Sarah's predictions before she died had stated exactly that.

"Sarah knew that a man would appear at the monastery and that he would bring with him the 'Seal of Sacred Virtue' " said the friar.

" 'The Seal of the Sacred Virtue'?" said Alex repeating his words.

"Yes, this is the name of the object you are talking about" nodded the friar, "and on the day that Sarah disappeared she was trying to bring it to me, but she never arrived. I only knew after many days, that she had been found dead near to Florence in the countryside."

"Exactly! In the countryside where Lunia lives – the young woman who saw the whole thing from the window of her house" explained Alex.

"So the Seal is in your hands?" asked the friar turning to face Alex.

"Yes and we safeguard it very well – don't worry." Alex responded reassuringly. "What we now have to do is work together closely, to throw more light on this story. I think it's going to be convenient for both of us, so tell me about the door, exactly where it is and what is actually behind that door" enquired Alex, anxious for an answer.

"My dear friend what you are asking me is to reveal the Greatest Secret of the Universe. It's not my job to talk to you about that secret. *"No man shall be able to reveal unto thee that which is hidden and the work of the Gods"*. You just have to be patient and you will understand along the path, exactly what it is. I, like you, don't have to know what is behind; not even Elizabeth or Sarah knew exactly what is hiding behind the Secret Door. I can only tell you, that there exists a map to reach it, but to reach it is not easy."

"And where is that map?" asked Alex

"The map to reach the door is accurately described in Elizabeth's diary where you can also read that she was endowed with messianic powers because she was the reincarnation of Queen Nefertiti of Ancient Egypt – the most beautiful woman who ever existed on this earth.

Elizabeth had this revelation when she was still a child, when she went to an unknown place with her father, asking him to dig into the ground because underneath there was an important finding.

So it was done, and they discovered the tomb of Queen Nefertiti, who had returned to Earth to give to humans knowledge of the Great Secret, that would liberate them from their bondage."

"Elizabeth's diary – where is it now?" asked Alex.

"It came back from where it was stolen" he responded with resentment.

"Exactly where?" asked Alex again.

"Exactly here! After someone from the congregation had the 'good idea' of handing it over to Hammed, the man who was working for Mr Bajin."

Alex felt suddenly baffled. Mr Bajin, the man who Alex had worked with, was one of the players of this story? It was intricate already but hopefully would become more clear with time.

The friar saw the upset on Alex's face and asked him "Did I say something wrong?"

"No everything is okay, it's just the name of Mr Bajin that upset me. I know that man, and to know that he belongs to this story puzzles me." Alex explained.

"He is just a materialistic person, who has taken advantage of the situation and tried to enrich himself, behind his partner Hammed as well: one more thief than the other" said the friar.

"So the diary is here with you?" queried Alex.

"Yes. I was handed it by the Chief of Police when they were recovering personal belongings from the hotel where Sarah was staying and they gave it to me" friar Sun explained.

"So the Chief of Police is also in the Congregation?" interrupted Alex.

"Yes he is one of our most important exponents, but if he now seems like a liar to you, please remember that he was also very helpful in guiding you to us. The man who stole the diary and the Seal from Hammed was a Principal of Sarah, or 'Sister Moon' as we called her.

She engaged this man, who belonged to the Congregation, to bring back the Seal, and to do that he had to pretend to work for both Mr Bajin and Hammed.

Years before, the diary had disappeared from the monastery where it had been guarded for centuries. We discovered later that the thief was a personal secretary of Sarah, who stole it and gave it directly to Hammed."

"For what reason did Sarah's secretary decide to steal the diary and give it to Hammed?" inquired Alex.

"Because he was at the end of his life through severe illness and he wanted to discover the Seal before his death but after several discussions with Sarah she repeatedly told him that it was not the right time. According to the diary Elizabeth said there would be a curse from Nefertiti if it was found before it's time."

"And when is the 'right time' according to the diary?" quizzed Alex.

"Nobody knows exactly when the 'right time' will be" Friar explained "But according with the diary which recorded the conversation between Queen Nefertiti and Elizabeth during one of her dreams, Sarah was waiting for some specific signs from the sky to establish the perfect moment. Unfortunately her secretary couldn't wait and became increasingly out of control from his illness, insisting that the time was right now."

The friar continued "And Hammed didn't waste any time in digging in the area indicated in the diary, where the Seal was hidden, but fortunately it was recovered by the Principal of Sarah. Unluckily, he was followed by someone who tracked down Sarah and killed her. You know the rest of the story, since it came into the hands of your friend Lunia. What we have to do now," he explained "is go to discover the place where the door is hidden, behind which there is a very valuable object."

"Yes I think we've got to the crossroads now, we just have to find the door;, hoping that somebody hasn't already arrived there before us" said Alex ironically.

"Yes indeed!" responded friar Sun.

Alex continued "As you know we are all involved in this intriguing story which has many crossing paths, sometimes without us even knowing why. I must confess I met Hammed who involved me in this whole mystery and because he has the ability to translate the ancient symbols, he is now committed to translate the ones we found recently inside the Seal."

"That news was expected" responded friar Sun "since Hammed was directly involved, having nearly been killed by one of Sarah's Adepts."

Alex then called Hammed "I have some good news as I found the diary which contains the information of the co-ordinates to reach the secret place that leads to the doorway".

"Well done young man!" Hammed exclaimed "I have good news for you too as I've just finished my translations of the symbols written on the metal tube from the Ankh. It seems to speak of an important object which is inside the door."

"Good! That is exactly what we were waiting for" added Alex encouragingly "And what do the translations say?"

"It says the object is something connected to energy in it's natural state which is neutral, but for some reason the energy can be altered. It all depends on many factors which are not yet clear." Then Hammed added, with growing concern in his voice "This object can enlighten the darkness of the consciousness but it has equally dark powers so, in my opinion, it can be something very dangerous. A blessing for humanity..."

"Or a curse?" added Alex.

"Perhaps." murmured Hammed, concluding the conversation.

As Alex put his phone away inside his jacket friar Sun spoke again. "It's time for you to know some important things, before you return to Luxor and the Sacred Place. It's about the people who, very intelligently left their tracks to make sure that we could find them again one day."

"Do you mean the Egyptian people?" asked Alex.

18

THE MASURITI

The Darkening

"I'm talking about the 'Masuriti' or 'People of the Gods'" said the friar. "They were people of Egyptian origin, who came from a branch of mysterious beings that arrived in Egypt many centuries before Christ, and no-one ever really knew where they came from. They were known as special people, with capacities that went far beyond the human limits. They had intuitive perception, to the point of being able to predict the long distant future, and in addition knew the past of anyone who came into contact with them. They had healing powers and are said to have travelled in time and space with specially advanced technological means."

"Are we talking about *'extra-terrestrials'*?" asked Alex somewhat incredulous to the words of this tale.

"For sure" said the friar. "It is said they came from Orion, the star which the ancient Egyptian devotees were convinced was precisely the identification of their God. And these people were the proof that they were the Gods from Orion, descended to the Earth, to save it from the dark evil that has concealed its light."

"And Elizabeth knew all these things, apparently?" asked Alex.

The friar elaborated "Elizabeth seems to be the daughter of a couple of archaeologists who were working in Egypt. Her father, one of the greatest exponents of the Masuriti people, was joined in marriage with a Lady of Scottish descent. Elizabeth knew of her extra-terrestrial origins, her father had always kept her informed of her own intuitive capabilities and tried to stimulate her into using these powers as a function of natural medicine. It seems that Elizabeth became a High Priestess of the Masuriti people, and that is the reason she was aware of the Great Secret that is now in our hands."

"And from what you tell me about Sarah" Alex probed "she was also endowed with extra-sensory powers?"

"Sarah was special, in everything she did" answered the friar shortly.

"I'm sorry. Maybe I shouldn't have asked" replied Alex noticing a veil of sadness descending on the man's face.

"That is a pain that will never heal until I accept the reason for her death" explained the friar sombrely.

"She was obviously a very important woman for you." stated Alex with concern.

"She was the first and last love of my life, and maybe something more" revealed the friar with the air of someone who finally rids themselves of a massive burden.

"Interesting! So you were in love with Sarah? And it mustn't have been easy to proceed this way as a friar?" said Alex, feeling sure that he was intent on continuing.

"As I already said, Sarah was the only true love of my life, and as such she will be forever. She was like her ancestor Elizabeth – both endowed with special powers, that went beyond the bounds of human comprehension. In short Sarah was Elizabeth, or rather her reincarnation. Like it or not, this is the reality. We all have a pathway to follow on this Earth, and this path does not end with life itself but continues in successive lifetimes, until it runs out and there is no need for the soul to reincarnate again.

Sarah was the reincarnation of Elizabeth, who in turn was the reincarnation of Queen Nefertiti. History has never sufficiently valued the identity of this Queen, who was actually the reincarnation of a divine Deity from the time of the Masuriti many centuries before. A pure, feminine energy that consecrated to Mother Earth as a pure spirit of nature, a generator and mother of all living beings here on Earth.

Sarah was aware of her divine origins. She often told me about her astral journeys, in which she saw the future of mankind in danger: a fact we now know, but there are some things still that no-one knows."

Alex was quite baffled by the friar's tale. He could no longer connect the real facts with the mystical truth which seemed to want to emerge from the very pores of that tale, so he decided to remain silent.

"Humanity was deceived from the very beginning" continued the friar "There are people who try every day to awaken this consciousness in humans, but it seems that there is still no sign of resumption, indeed..." the friar paused and gave a long sigh "almost everyone is completely kidnapped by the hypnotic effect of evil that dominates our planet, controlled by a few beings disguised as humans, but in reality they are cool and calculating, and operating behind the scenes of the social system, creating fictitious illusions directed towards mass control through a system of psychophysical intoxication, which no-one is yet aware of."

"And who are these so-called 'people' who operate behind the scenes of the social system?" asked Alex.

"We do not know them directly, but they are those who educate our Politicians; who are also abducted at an unconscious level, and reduced to being puppets in their hands." explained the friar.

"So it is not the politicians who govern the laws of a country? And the people vote in Parliamentarians who do not exist to represent their ideals in this society?" finished Alex.

The friar continued "This is the least of our problems, it is just to create the classic 'smoke in the eyes' to confuse people, but now the truth will be revealed because there is a lack of consistency between fact and opinions, so people inevitably start to make questions that have spread in recent years, to all the countries of the world.

As you may have noticed, many countries are very similar to each other, and adopt the same rules that control their governmental systems. The entire system is unique from a socio-political standpoint and is aimed at selecting people from social classes, so the poor become ever poorer and the rich get richer still.

The aim is to eradicate those who are regarded as useless: the poor who are now unsupported from the capitalistic system, which no longer needs this mass of people to achieve their aims. The system now produces more, but with technological advances which have replaced work forces, and these products are aimed at a different group of consumers: the young, as easily manipulated, but continually reduced in terms of quantity, so this tends to create a society where younger people no longer work to pay the pensions of the elderly.

So the elderly are eliminated before they enter that social band of 'retirement', saving a lot of money that has been invested in secretive weapons, ready to destroy a community as large as Europe. The only awareness of that power, is the continual need to fight and negotiate from country to country under the pressure of blackmail.

The people who orchestrate this process, are the prime antagonists of the Masuriti, coming from the same planet as them, but at a much later stage of development, when Orion was overshadowed by the light because the people moved away spiritually, from their true paths.

The Sun could no longer penetrate into their aquifers, and the vegetation was reduced to dry foliage, and the air became arid, as arid also became their souls. Defenceless in an atmosphere without divine light, the living beings of their society that had once been created to be in harmony with nature and in contact with the light, had been struck by the evil of the darkening, which saw many of them transmute into monstrous-looking, cold-hearted beings who fed on blood and violence.

Some beings from the Masuriti society managed to save themselves, and descended to Earth to rebuild an ideal life here that was based on the divine principles that once existed on Orion. But unfortunately amongst their community hid infected beings who transformed to become true killers, ready to suck the blood of their neighbours in the night, as true vampires do. And so the

Masuriti society became two opposing factions on Earth – the 'White Masuriti' and the 'Black Masuriti'."

"Where did you get all this precious information?" wondered Alex.

Friar Sun elaborated "Everything I've told you comes from Elizabeth's diary who, as I said, was in contact with the divine. And that allowed her to visualise what she needed to know and record it in her diary to let future human beings know what was happening. Sarah was an inheritor of the diary and she reported to me after reading it and developing her own knowledge through it."

Then the friar broke off from his story and Alex realised it was now time to go beyond the past history, and instead to find the oracle that may be hiding behind the door in the city of Luxor, and they both decided to go and investigate the secret door, that the Seal of Sacred Virtues would open.

They began by scrutinising the map that was in Elizabeth's diary. The map was secret and needed to be interpreted by those who knew the language of the Masuriti. Friar Sun knew the laws that had founded their society, but didn't know the difficult interpretation so accurately described in ancient hieroglyphics which, centuries later, evolved into the society of the Egyptians.

The roots of the language of the Masuriti were traceable back to scientific codes that were interpreted as a language based on the arrangements of the planetary systems. It was therefore clear that they knew far more than today's official scientific world which still struggles to calculate, despite our sophisticated computer technology, and by comparison they were and still are vastly inferior to the means that the Masuriti had available to them.

Friar Sun therefore decided to consult one of his followers who had the role of interpreter of ancient languages within the community; an expert in Karmic and Esoteric Astrology. That character was named friar Sky but his real name was Peter Obram from Texas, and he came to Italy for the sake of scientific research where he met friar Sun at an astrological conference and agreed to move to his monastery with the task of studying the Masuriti society and their mysteries.

Friar Sky was delighted for the chance to interpret the map that was outlined in Elizabeth's diary so accurately, and after a careful examination that compelled him to be secluded for more than a day, he summoned them for a preview of the first findings that he had made. They listened quietly to the long awaited interpretation, that might lead them to the secret door.

"The map leads to a place in the ancient city of Iunet (the one that's called Dendra city today) which in

Arabic means Goddess. It is here where one of the most exactly preserved Temples can be found – the Temple of Dendra, previously known as the Temple of the Goddess Hathor as it was dedicated to her in the Roman Greek era" friar Sky reported. "In this temple there is hidden the Secret of the Oracle."

"Dendra Temple is only sixty kilometres north of Luxor so we can use it as a base to start from" suggested Alex.

The two friars nodded in agreement.

19

LUNIA

No Escape

Lunia had returned to her daily life, leaving Alex to continue his investigations that would soon be brought back to the magical atmosphere of ancient Egypt where, for a while, she had been able to live that short but intense adventure that made her an important protagonist of those intriguing enigmas rich in mystery and suspense; however she didn't know how to reach a finale that would satisfy her thirst to learn more.

But someone had not forgotten about her and had already decided to recall her once more into the centre of this mysterious adventure, where she was inevitably entwined and perhaps the artificer, who could not escape from her destiny.

It was during one of the following nights when she was completely alone in her bedroom that she suddenly heard strange noises coming from the cornfield surrounding the house. Lunia was startled and made her way quickly to the window; that same window from which, too many times, she had already seen so many strange things. But this time she saw no one except the usual shadows of the trees, ghosts that moved their fronds to the breath of the wind that hissed as if it was part of a scream that was coming from afar; like the voices of those who claim vengeance and who want to take back what belongs to them:

"Lunia! Lunia!" she seemed to hear in the call of the wind. But in fact it was just her fantasy – the one that usually kept her awake during the night when her dreams were crossing with reality, giving her the opportunity to access her highest level of creativity, where boundaries dissolve into the absurdity and impossibility of controlling the unseen.

The door of the house was closed but someone had managed to open it and now he was climbing the stairs. Lunia was completely vulnerable in her bed without any possibility of escaping, like the time the man had come in to look for the infamous Seal. This time Lunia felt lost and knew that she would shortly come face to face with the suspected murderer. The slow but deliberate steps marked the seconds, counting away the time from what could potentially be the end of her young life. Then Lunia began to travel in that astral world where ghosts of the past come to greet to make the moment of passing more sweet, from what we normally define as a material life to what we imagine is the spiritual one.

So Lunia saw childhood moments with her grandparents and her big family in the country house, the fields of flowers in the beloved spring, the fruit of the trees in the countryside where grandma spent her days cultivating the land while she looked at her - trying to imitate her and all her little ways that made her feel grown up. She saw her parents and in particular her mother who with a tender smile told her not to be afraid and to grow, and that all was well, but that life was not as simple as playing with dolls. Prince Charming would not come as easily as she had imagined and many such Princes would arrive in her dreams as a young woman but many of them would fall long before reaching the castle and the right one would come when she at last would leave open the door of her heart!

Lunia had never understood why the heart should have a door and why she had never been given the keys to open it, but she certainly knew that her heart was full of love and she just needed to learn how to keep it safe from those who would damage it.

At that moment, however she did not care more about the door of the heart but of the door of the house which had mysteriously opened up, putting her life in serious imminent danger. The man reached the door of her bedroom. She was in the darkness of the deepest silence, where she dare not even take a breath. The handle moved slowly to open the closed door when on the other side, the impatient man began to speak:

"Open the door Lunia. I know you're in there. Or I will open it myself!"

She was frightened and suddenly wished that Alex was there so she didn't have to face this moment of terror alone. She tried to phone him but he didn't answer, so, in panic she left a whispered message:

"Alex I'm in serious danger. Someone's got into the house and is at my locked bedroom door. I hope I get out but if I don't I want you to know that you have been very important to me. I wish I could meet you again to continue this adventurous journey and the great discoveries which you are destined to make.

I was hoping, maybe one day that you could be a bigger part of my life, one that I had always dreamed of. Goodbye!" Then she put the phone down in a safe corner pushing the record button so it might record some of the murderers voice.

The door suddenly swung open. The man had forced it without too much effort. He stood by the door, trying to locate in the darkness where the young woman might be. He finally found the switch to a faint lamp placed on the bedside table. The bed was empty but he could still feel the warmth of a body that had definitely laid there a few moments before.

"Lunia come out! You've got no chance!" shouted the man firmly, in a foreign accent. Then an elusive shadow seemed to quickly pass through his body, flying like a phantom that slammed the door abruptly behind him. It was Lunia who was desperately trying to reach the bathroom door from where she knew she would be able to escape once more through the ceiling hatch, but this time the man reached out and grabbed her before she could reach it and Lunia suddenly knew she had no way to escape.

20

ALEX

Returning to Egypt

As soon as they arrived in Egypt the three men would head towards Luxor and Jabril's house from where, following the directions held in Elizabeth's diary, they would continue towards Iunet. When Alex walked towards the terminal building he received Lunia's message which was sent to him when his phone was off. The two friars saw from Alex's face that something had shocked him.

"Lunia is in danger!" exclaimed Alex loudly "And I don't know if she's still alive!" he continued, in a very confused state.

Friar Sky and friar Sun, shocked by this news, don't hesitate to ask Alex what he is talking about, as Alex quickly phones Lunia hoping to find out if she will answer. But Lunia doesn't respond and the phone appears to be switched off so Alex leaves a message in the hope that she will still receive it.

Alex spoke clearly into his phone "Lunia please call me as soon as you can otherwise I will have to contact Police. I am waiting for your news."

Jabril was waiting for them and as soon as they arrived he immediately knew from Alex's face that something had gone wrong. But the happiness of seeing that young archaeologist with such kind and captivating looks that recalled his Latin origins made Jabril feel suddenly full of life. Jabril had never confessed to Alex his true feelings for him but Alex had understood and had always been equally fascinated.

The idea of being at the centre of Jabril's attention, which already from their time together at university had manifested itself on many occasions, made him reflect many times, during his existential crisis, about his identity and his personal preferences. And now with Jabrils face in front of him Alex suddenly felt that of course this was the right way, however uncertain and different. It would inevitably lead him to question his identity but certainly would be more honest than he would have been in trying to hide it.

21

LUNIA

The Revelation

The man blocked Lunia's way and kept her stuck to the floor in front of the bathroom that she was trying so hard to reach. He covered her mouth, preventing her from screaming and as she struggled for breath her spoke to her firmly:

"I'm not here to kill you, I just want to talk to you about something very important."

Then Lunia quietened down and slowly let her body relax under the heavy pressure of his large muscular arms.

"I'm here to pick up the Seal that belongs to Sarah. I know that you found it but it has to get back into the right hands before it's too late" said the man with the air of someone who was clear about what he wanted.

Lunia felt confused because she had believed the man to be the same one who, days before, had managed to enter the house and leave the letter which had become her invitation to go to Egypt.

"Who are you then?" asked Lunia with a little voice that was still suffocated by fear.

"My name is Hassan. I am Egyptian but I have lived in Italy for a long time since I joined the Spiritual Congregation of which Sarah was the leader. I served until the day of her tragic death as she tried to protect the Seal but unfortunately she was killed before she could deliver it to friar Sun.

Sarah ordered me to retrieve the Seal from Hammed in the Great Pyramid when he planned to remove it. Sarah also left a papyrus to be found later by Alex, which was written by her in hieroglyphic language. She told me to put it in the rock box where Alex found it.

The papyrus had a message in it that showed a route leading to Luxor. She had seen, in one of her premonition dreams, where she had seen people, including you and Alex, who would meet in Luxor to plan the finding of the mysterious object that lurks behind the Sacred Door of the Temple of Dendra at Iunet.

That day I obviously couldn't let Hammed recognise me, so I hit him on the head and took the Seal and Elizabeth's diary from his hands. Unfortunately as soon as I hit him there was a great landslide in the area that reached the room of the Great Pyramid.

I managed to escape before the landslide hit me too but that left Hammed as the victim in this incident, and he still pays the consequences today, being completely paralysed in the legs. It has been written since ancient times that anyone who attempted to profane the Great Pyramid should suffer a curse for the rest of their life."

"So who killed Sarah and why?" Lunia asked, rather marvelled after listening to Hassan who was slowly reassuring her by revealing a completely different aspect of himself to the one she had assumed during his initial intrusion.

"I delivered the diary and the Seal to Sarah who at that time was here in Italy" Hassan explained. "She should have delivered the Seal to friar Sun but someone from the congregation did not agree with Sarah's idea of continuing to keep the Seal hidden and not to proceed until the right moment was revealed by the great spirit guide Queen Nefertiti, who was still in communication with Elizabeth.

These three women linked together were the key to guarding the secret that hides behind the door of that Holy Place."

"Who was this person who didn't agree?" enquired Lunia.

"This man was Sarah's trusted secretary. He tried to take away the Seal but couldn't find it because it was in your hands." Hassan continued "Sarah had begun to doubt her secretary, who was given the name of friar Fire by the Congregation during his initiation ceremony where members swear to serve the Congregation and its missionary purposes. Friar Fire was so called because of his strength and temperance and he had, on several recent occasions, quarrelled animatedly with Sarah.

This is how she lost faith in him and decided to prevent what actually happened by commissioning me to bring the Seal to Italy where friar Sun would have guarded it until the day that Sarah would decide, after receiving a mystical order by seeing it in her dream, when it would be the right time.

Sarah received her order to proceed in this mission by following precise steps dictated in the diary by the spirit of Elizabeth who, in turn, was in contact with Queen Nefertiti.

That day, friar Fire didn't agree with her plan and in his fury he decided to steal the Seal from Sarah's hands when he picked her up from the airport, knowing that she had it in her purse. He decided to change direction by bringing Sarah into the countryside where he thought he could take the Seal from her without anyone seeing, but he hadn't taken into account what fate had prepared instead. And that's how you appeared on the scene – the rest you know" he concluded.

"So Sarah would have been killed by friar Fire, her secretary?" wondered Lunia becoming even more surprised by what Hassan was telling her.

"Sarah had confessed to me that she had seen in a dream, that something dangerous was about to happen but didn't know quite what it was about. And she told me that if anyone attempted to take the Seal before it was handed over to friar Sun she would have to kill herself to save the secret of the mysterious object behind the door that someone would try to steal.

We still don't know what happened that day when Sarah died. The investigations are still underway for her murder." said the man with a trickle of uncertainty that reflected his own inner doubts.

"And where is friar Fire now? As it was him who came here the first time to take the Seal and left me the letter inviting me to go to Egypt" asked Lunia

"Friar Fire is still in the Congregation and under investigation by them and the Police since he was the last person to have seen Sarah alive, having collected her from the airport" Hassan explained. "He is still saying that he left her in front of the monastery of friar Sun where she was meant to deliver the Seal but where she never actually arrived."

"So the story gets a lot more intriguing than I thought" said Lunia, pretty excited to be still in the middle of an ongoing adventure.

"If you like complicated stories then you are definitely in the right one" ended Hassan with a smile that indicated to her the desire to remain friendly.

22

ALEX

Prince Charming

It was when Alex felt released from doubts that assaulted his mind regarding Jabril, that on his phone finally appeared Lunia's name as she was calling him. He gave a sigh of relief at seeing that she was still apparently alive and so hastened to reply to her.

"Lunia you really made me worried with that message. Where are you? Are you all right?" said Alex, still thinking of Jabril who a few moments before had occupied in his mind that space of the most hidden secrets.

"Yes Alex I'm alright" Lunia responded "and everything's fine but I need to talk to you about very important things regarding the Seal" and that's when Lunia told him about Hassan and all that he had revealed to her, especially about the truth of the papyrus that Alex had found in the Great Pyramid and the reasons why Sarah had planned to have it found in the right place at the right time in order for them both to be connected.

Alex was amazed as he listened to the detailed story that Lunia was telling him and he felt guilty for doubting Hammed, having accused him several times of putting the papyrus in the Great Pyramid to divert them from the traces of the Secret Door by directing them to Luxor and not Iunet as it had been written by Elizabeth in her diary.

Then Lunia lingered for a moment, thinking of the contents of the message that she had sent to Alex the day before in which the fear of death had given her the courage to confess the passion she cultivated during that time for the young American archaeologist with Latin origins, a wish that Lunia had set aside in her dream world where, once again, she should have seen it fail: the Myth of her Prince Charming.

There were moments of silence in which they both listened to their breaths then they each ended the conversation with 'See you later' knowing that this was actually 'goodbye' when Alex suddenly hinted at wanting to continue the conversation maybe because he didn't like 'goodbyes' or perhaps, once again, he wished to clarify his doubts but when he realised that the other side of the conversation was ended as Lunia hung up, he felt relieved for those words never said and that they would never find an answer in the days to come.

23

DENDRA TEMPLE

The Secret Door

Alex and the two friars headed to Dendra Temple. Once they entered, they followed the instructions that friar Sky had thoroughly prepared for them, to follow what was a path which would lead them to a place where the Oracle dwelt.

Friar Sky led them in front of one of the most important symbols that characterised the temple. It was represented by a bas-relief, carved in stone, the famous Zodiac that according to the different interpretations, could be traced back to the Roman empire, and it represented a sky map dated to 4500 years before Christ - so long before the Egyptian civilisation, conceived probably by the people of the Masuriti.

Then friar Sky carefully took out the 'Seal of the Sacred Virtue' which was made in gold bas-relief, carved to match the same contours of the lock. So it was supposed to be the key to the opening of the door, behind which lurked the secret that they yearned for, for so long. Months of intense adventures and long research had led the three men, bound by the same destiny, to the discovery of a mysterious object, and awareness of the Ultimate Reality that would change the destiny of men on Earth.

The Seal was the key, but it was necessary to find the door following the instructions translated from the map. Friar Sky walked on the right side of the temple, then he turned behind the Zodiac and reached a very dark area characterised by majestic colonnades and passages intersecting each other, as a labyrinth, where it was easy to become disorientated, but friar Sky seemed to be sure where he was going, and Alex, with Friar Sun, followed him confidently towards that branch of tunnels, between one column and another. Then at one point friar Sky suddenly stopped and seemed to be listening to some distant noise; it could have been the sound of a voice, or maybe he was just pondering to look for the exact spot.

In the silence of the evening the air was fresh, but the wind from the warm desert arrived at the river and became, at certain times of the day, like music accompanied by a supreme chant of an ancient mantra, that fascinated anyone who stopped to listen to its intensity, full of mystery and profound peace.

And it was at that instant, that friar Sky walked to an exact spot between the majestic colonnade of the temple, and vanished into obscurity, as if he had been sucked into a black hole. Alex and friar Sun didn't believe their eyes. The man who a few moments before was just ahead of them, had vanished into thin air, without leaving any traces of himself.

"How is it possible?" Alex marvelled.

"I have no idea where he disappeared to!" replied friar Sun.

The two men made a desperate search attempt by calling out for him, listening from time to time for any response, but with the knowledge that friar Sky had vanished completely for some strange reason, which perhaps had brought him to a place of no return.

24

ESOTERIC SCIENCE

Alchemy of the Spirit

"What do we do?" asked Alex desperately as his eyes continued to search for some sign of the missing friar.

"Maybe we should consult Elizabeth's diary for an answer?" suggested friar Sun as he pulled the precious book from his rucksack, holding it aloft for Alex to see. "In here she describes in detail the mystery of ESOTERIC SCIENCE and how an explanation of certain phenomena of transshipment and disappearance of bodies and objects. The subject was exactly known as dematerialisation of body, defined as spiritual alchemy that for some people is found only in fairy tales."

"Well" said Alex "Let's see what the diary tells us about spiritual alchemy" and he moved to join friar Sun as he opened the diary to the section detailing how certain bodies can dematerialise and re-materialise elsewhere.

"It's very interesting" reassured friar Sun "and it can give us some pointers to understand the disappearance of friar Sky."

"We hope" blurted Alex "otherwise we will have to say goodbye forever without even knowing where his body has gone."

Friar Sun continued "The diary says this:

*The **'ALCHEMY OF THE SPIRIT'** – It requires first of all the esoteric knowledge of our body in the face of the entire Universe speaking of the Natural Law that characterises the Micro-Macrocosm, and for that principle we must bear in mind that our body is the same as the Universe in terms of molecular structure. We are therefore a set of small coexisting Universes within the interior of an even greater one and therefore we are guided by the same Law of Attraction that regulates the planets that in our body are nothing more than the nuclei of our cells.*

We are therefore composed of so many small solar systems, placed in each single cell. Understanding the Universe and its origins is the first step to understanding ourselves. Lets start at the point where the Universe was born by the explosion of a star that gave rise to the planets. (Big Bang Theory).

MICRO-MACROCOSM: "The Breath of the Universe" *- When such explosive energy was generated by the divine CREATIVE FORCE called 'GOD', that at some point could no longer be contained and had the need to expand itself through this EXPLOSION. Then the EXPANSION of it outwards, which is a form of*

LOVE that manifests itself from a single body, generated by the desire to GIVE of itself and then to CREATE (procreation of children) the UNIVERSE, that once exploded, had the need to return to its CENTRE, driven by the law of gravity generated by the EXPLOSION as an EXPANSION and IMPLOSION back to the CENTRE, like in the MICROCOSM when we take a BREATH.

Our every exhaled breath is an outward explosion which is then gathered inwards as an inhalation towards the interior of our being. We can therefore say that as a human, forming part of the Universe, we are guided by the same energy that regulates this GENERATING MOVEMENT, which in the MACROCOSM gave rise to the planets, and in the MICROCOSM gives rise to our breath, which is tuned to the beating of our heart. At each beat bursts an explosion and then there is an implosion that, in our bodies, is the recollection of blood pumping through the veins towards the heart.

Who could not confirm, at this point that the explosion of the star (BIG BANG) and it's subsequent implosion, which occurred so many millions of years ago in the past and is ready to repeat again, is nothing more than the beating of a big heart? Precisely, the heart of God that moves in harmony with our heart, and that its breath is nothing more than our breath, by the Law of Synchronicity, and it is thereby that we find the coexistence of human with God in the Universe, expressed over time through dances like Sufi dance, where the body, mind and soul are connected by the same wavelength and then, through the dance, they tune in harmony.

In Sufi dance the symbolic movements of displacement, from a central point outwards, have a profound meaning of DONATION and INTEGRATION, (moving outwards) and RECOLLECTION (moving inwards), to emphasise RECONNECTION WITH ONESELF (back to the centre).

Following the elements that regulate life, we can understand those that regulate death. The one who does not give himself and therefore does not follow the rules of expansion, does not regenerate himself because he does not give oxygen to the spirit, and therefore not even to his own body, and consequently he folds in on himself, slowly turning off (depression), and eventually disconnection, degenerating himself in his emptiness.

The origin of many degenerative diseases often arise from this negative attitude; from having focused too much on themselves, and not enough on others (greed); for refusing to generate children, for having been afraid of the responsibilities that life requires, and also for the illusion of protecting themselves by isolation when in reality the energy needs to expand to regenerate itself. Those people believe that they can protect their materialistic property like food, money, homes without expanding their body, and therefore their spirit, so they do not generate more antibodies, but rather develop degenerative disease of the body and the mind.

Humanity needs to change its concept of living in permanence on this planet. It needs to acquire the consciousness of its own existence by following the movement which regulates the Universe, tuning with it, otherwise in time it will be extinguished for not being useful, instead of being an obstacle to the life dance, which needs harmony through fluency of the energy (Peace) and not the contrast which creates blockages (Anger, Resentment).

Then the Human (Microcosm) to be in harmony with the Universe (Macrocosm) which it belongs to, needs to follow the movement of EXPLOSION (Expansion, Donation, Creation, Generosity) and IMPLOSION (Recollection, Meditation, Consciousness of Self) to be in tune with the natural balance as a font of Vital Energy. So illness is a sign for our body, recalling what we need to do to return to balance. We are the architects of our destiny and also of our illness, we generate life but also death, we can donate ourself but we can also destroy ourself.

To maintain a good psychophysical base it is necessary to work on Vital Energy which goes through our body on the physical plane and through our mind on the mental plane and then in our spirit on the spiritual plane. All these planes are part of our being which from the materialistic body, projects itself onto the thinner planes until it reaches the spiritual one. There are seven planes for each human body, surrounding us like shells from the thickest to the thinnest, from the physical to the spiritual which is our essence.

*The **VITAL ENERGY** which connects all these planes has a vertical path and expands itself upwards through the centres of energy named CHAKRAS. This energy in the Sanskrit language is known as KUNDALINI ENERGY which runs up the spinal chord of the physical body and connects to the endocrine glands through thin invisible energetic lines called Nadi. The Kundalini then, is our energy that regulates all of our vital planes and connects all of them at one spiritual point which is above all living beings, the one we call God.*

"Very interesting. However we still didn't find out how to find our friend friar Sky" said Alex speaking to friar Sun while looking into the empty space around them for some kind of sign.

Friar Sun brought his attention back to Elizabeth's diary and continued reading:

Then the Vital Energy runs through the chakras and via the mind can reach the body focusing on the seven vital points of our body corresponding to the lymph or endocrine glands. For that reason it's necessary for the energy to run fluently through the chakras otherwise it becomes blocked and that's how illness is created in the body and the mind. To make that energy have a flowing course, the mind must function well and also be fluent in formulating positive thoughts. In this regard it is necessary first of all to be aware of all this, and therefore of ourselves at the energetic level.

When we are aware not only of our own abilities but also of our own limitations, we can imagine ourselves (or better still our energetic body) as a lake that easily ripples, even with a single puff of wind or with a stone thrown into it. These are the emotions that act on our energetic body, just like the pebble in the lake ruffling its surface. And of course the bigger the rock, the more the water becomes rippled (emotions), but then it becomes calm and flat once again, whilst being vulnerable even to a single breath of wind. So our energy is exactly like the lake, but if we are aware of it, we can apply a rule, which is also the secret to finding the balancing point: 'follow the water movement and do not thwart its movement, but get in tune and flow with it'. A bit like when you ride a horse and become an integral part of its body and its movement, and thus synchronise yourself with its flowing energy field.

Emotional synchronicity with our energy field occurs when emotions are processed and transformed with understanding and acceptance, and become flexible to that movement that transforms into a dance with our energetic body, living in balance with it, and consequently with everything else around us (harmony). All this is the principle of Alchemy; the first step towards TRANSFORMATION. We do not die, but we simply transform ourselves, and for that we can travel from one body to another in different dimensions.

There are people who never abandon the physical body, but disappear into thin air and in this mystery they leave a great void for those who remain and do not know where they have gone. For reasons that are not yet clear, they leave the physical dimension to enter the atomic dimension without abandoning the body, so they are no longer visible to the human eye, and they are still present but they don't know how to find their way back.

There are techniques to help those who have disappeared, to regain their physical dimensions and integrate with it. The secret is in the mental concentration of those who call it to attention. If the one who has disappeared receives the message, they can find the way back and return.

(And then there were listed the different steps to practice this concentration.)

"At this point" said Alex "there is nothing left to do but to try to bring friar Sky back by practising this teaching."

So the two went back to the point where friar Sky had disappeared, and the practice of concentration began.

"You need to close your eyes and breathe deeply" said friar Sun reading the instructions "Then listen to the beating of your heart and tune in with it. Keep breathing deeply and listen to your breath. Tune even with your breath. Open your arms upwards in the pose of receiving, by looking for the point which is the centre of gravity: the exact point where you feel that your raised arms do not need any effort, and feel totally supported. Then relax.

Then start to emit the sacred sound 'AOUM', starting the sound from the centre of the diaphragm and allow the sound to vibrate the pancreas gland or solar plexus chakra. Allow the sound to climb up lightly and change to the 'U' stage which makes the transition to the 'M' stage much smoother.

Then let the 'U' vibrate in the centre of the throat, corresponding to the thyroid gland or throat chakra and then go up to the centre of the head, making the pineal gland vibrate with the sound of the 'M', extending it until the end of the breath and concentrate on the vibration. Start again with a deep breath from the diaphragm, towards the head and repeat all of this at least ten times."

And so they both did this until they tuned in to the energy of the place. Then friar Sun began to speak, keeping his eyes closed and his arms in the position of receiving from above.

"I can see a shadow.... of a man walking towards us...."

"I can see it too!" said Alex "I cannot see the face but from how he walks I think it is friar Sky!"

"Yes that's exactly him!" repeated friar Sun.

"Well, let's tune in with him and maybe we can bring him back" said Alex.

And so they let the man approach close enough to be able to clearly see his face. The man walked slowly and looked around as if trying to figure out where he was and what was happening to him, looking among the pillars of the Temple as if to seek the way back. Then Alex was able to hear his voice; it was dim and far away but in the time that the figure approached them even the voice grew louder until he was able to hear his name:

"Alex? Where are you?" shouted the man.

Alex gasped but he restrained himself, following friar Sun's lead who had read in the diary that as soon as he heard the voice he should be silent to avoid the person being disturbed or frightened, otherwise his energetic body would vanish forever; it was therefore a very delicate phase they were going through, and their actions in the next few moments would determine whether this game would be won or lost, because it was dominated by unknown forces that put into play the destiny of a man who was riding between two dimensions.

And maybe not just him, but all of humanity who, without being aware of it, were about to be awakened to a new level of consciousness that would change the fate of all the humans of the Earth towards unknown horizons, and for that reason was potentially dangerous. Everything was in the hands of the little alchemic knowledge that Alex and friar Sun had.

They were working to bring back a man from an unknown place, following Elizabeth's instructions, who, as much as they knew, was just a simple archaeologist researcher of a world that for centuries had mysteriously characterised the Egyptian people.

Now they were there, in the place where centuries before other people had also mysteriously disappeared and never returned. And also where strange-looking people also appeared like the Masuriti, coming from another planet without any obvious transport by simply crossing the threshold from another dimension which had passage to an exact point between the pillars of the Temple.

That was the famous door they were looking for, and the key or the 'Seal of the Sacred Virtue' was the symbol of Eternity, '8', where it was possible to gain access, only with knowledge of alchemic practices. But with the irony of destiny, some people were sucked in without any will on their part. Maybe it was a chemical combination that allowed the opening of this tunnel where these people disappeared in front of the eyes of others?

There was talk of many archaeologists who had mysteriously disappeared in that place in the past. Someone had argued that they had been kidnapped by the mysterious people of the Masuriti for energetic experimental purposes, or to steal the identity they needed to gain access to colonisation on planet Earth.

No-one knew, but Elizabeth had learned of many mysteries that would open new horizons for a new world, where human beings would acquire the knowledge of their true nature and therefore of the freedom that had been occulted to enslave human beings under the power of the Black Masuriti; those who had remained in the darkness of a vampire planet and fed on fear as an energetic form of survival.

Once they had found out where friar Sky was, the two men stopped meditating and returned into their body, leaving him to wander in that place for a while longer. Hopefully they would be able to reconnect with him later, after having read some more of the invaluable instructions given to them in the diary by Elizabeth. Then they walked again, without any exact goal, looking for an answer to that mystery between the walls of a temple that had them imprisoned for now.

"Okay" exclaimed Alex "we've made contact with him. How do we bring him back here?"

"Let me read the diary to see if it gives us any more information" replied friar Sun.

It was almost by accident that Alex stopped to look up at the sky that stood over the majestic colonnades of the Temple, when he caught sight, on one of the gigantic pillars, of a bas-relief that vaguely resembled the 'Key of Sacred Virtue' that Alex, now almost hopeless, had nearly forgotten to have with him in his custody.

"Look up there!" said Alex to friar Sun pointing his finger upwards.

"I don't see anything" said friar Sun.

"There is a symbol carved on the right side at the top of the column here, in front of us" said Alex. Friar Sun was struggling to see from so far away, but had confidence in what Alex had said he'd seen.

Alex continued "We must be able to frame the Seal of the Sacred Virtues at that exact point. I'm sure that is the key to opening the door we were looking for!" and while he was saying this Alex had the vision of friar Sky who was still wandering in the other dimension, searching for a way out. "Friar Sky may return, if we help him open that door, but we must make sure that he can take the key, and indicate to him where he has to insert it."

With concentrated alignment, the two were now back in touch with their lost friend and when they were certain that friar Sky was finally on the same wavelength. Alex started the first steps to get in touch with him, being careful not to provoke any wave interference that would separate them forever. It began with a subtle and delicate tone that flowed from the belly to the mouth, emanating from the sacred sound of 'AOUM'.

Friar Sky began to perceive that sound and they saw him trying to figure out where it came from. Then Alex started whispering his name "Friar Sky! We're here!"

The man began to clearly perceive his name and recognised Alex's voice.

"I hear you! I hear you Alex! Where are you?" he called out.

"I'm right next to you but you can't see me!" Alex replied.

So friar Sky understood that he had entered into another dimension, and his heart began to beat more quickly, and he began to panic. Alex watched as he saw friar Sky's figure slowly fade, so that only his contour was left. Friar Sky's panic was emitting contrasting vibrations that were too strong, and friar Sun and Alex were beginning to lose contact with him.

"This is explained by Elizabeth in her diary" said friar Sun and he continued to read:

When the figure of the one who is absorbed by the Astral Dimension weakens in the eyes of those who come into contact with it, it means the magnetic field has suffered conflicting vibrations, and they can vanish into thin air.

This is the most delicate and dangerous phase. In this case it is necessary to re-establish a balance of the energy field between the one who is within the ASTRAL dimension and those who are in the MATERIAL plane.

Alex also had moments when panic arose within him, and his instinct was to run towards his friend to drag him back into matter, but he restrained himself and, with a deep breath, resumed control of the situation. Friar Sun perceived the danger, but let Alex guide the situation, avoiding any unnecessary and dangerous interference. Alex started again to talk calmly, and tried to visualise the face of friar Sky that was slowly disappearing.

"Stay calm. Sit down and breathe slowly, and listen to me without fear, and you will return to the matter very soon" said friar Sun, to recover what little was left of his frightened friend.

At these words friar Sky quietened himself and sat down with his bewildered eyes looking about him, still trying to figure out where friar Sun's voice came from.

Alex intervened by following the instructions from the diary "Right, now follow my instructions. Go to your right and look up. On a column there is carved a symbol which is the key to re-entering the matter. But you must first be able to take the Seal of the Sacred Virtue, which is still here with me. To take it, you have to close your eyes and return into yourself and view the object, then try to touch it, and finally take it. Eventually, it will materialise between your hands, and you should reach a point at the top of the column where the Seal can be placed exactly inside the bas-relief. At that point you will return into matter."

Then Alex placed the key onto a central point of the Temple, between the two columns leading to the Purification Chapel, where according to the instructions it would be transmitted to the other dimension, from where friar Sky could finally open the Sacred Door.

Once he positioned the key, Alex sat down at one side in a meditative position, then he closed his eyes, and reconnected with friar Sky, and he saw him slowly moving towards where the key had been placed.

When Alex saw friar Sky take the Seal, he opened his eyes to see if it was still there, but instead it was gone: it had entered into the other dimension, and now it was in the hands of friar Sky. Then he closed his eyes again, and saw friar Sky rising slowly from the ground, incredibly fluent; he had achieved the ability to fly!

Then once he had reached the highest point of the column, he placed the key inside the bas-relief, and a blinding light dazzled the sight of Alex, and although he failed to see exactly what happened, a few moments later he saw friar Sky with a papyrus in his hand, walking towards him.

Alex re-opened his eyes and saw his friend standing there in front of him, healthy and well, and full of light; a light that came from somewhere within him and emanated from all of his pores, illuminating even his eyes. As he greeted them both with a smile full of joy, friar sky embraced his two friends, still incredulous in seeing him there, but so happy to know that their mission had succeeded.

25

THE THREE VISIONS

The Line - The Circle - The Spiral

They chatted long together about their incredible story, that would later become the news of the century "TRANSSHIPMENT TO ANOTHER DIMENSION": the beginning of a new era, which was one that allowed travel through parallel Universes by thought and molecular decomposition. They had in hand the right ingredients for a unique recipe, that would bring about a new world, but they still didn't yet know how to use those ingredients to create a real-life status that would apply on planet Earth, now in full conflict and destruction.

The three talked together of their experience, and still in a state of incredulity friar Sky spoke with great serenity of his journey, which he called 'the most interesting and fascinating journey a human being can make' but very often the most mysterious and dangerous journey is the round trip with no return.

When questions from Alex and friar Sun had run out, friar Sky showed them the papyrus that he had found at the point of the Seal where the Key of Sacred Virtue had struck the column. It was an ancient manuscript, written in the language of the Masuriti. Friar Sky perfectly translated its title as 'The Three Visions of

Life'. It describes how human beings are divided into different thought form groups, with three particular 'Visions'.

'The First Vision' was called 'THE LINE'

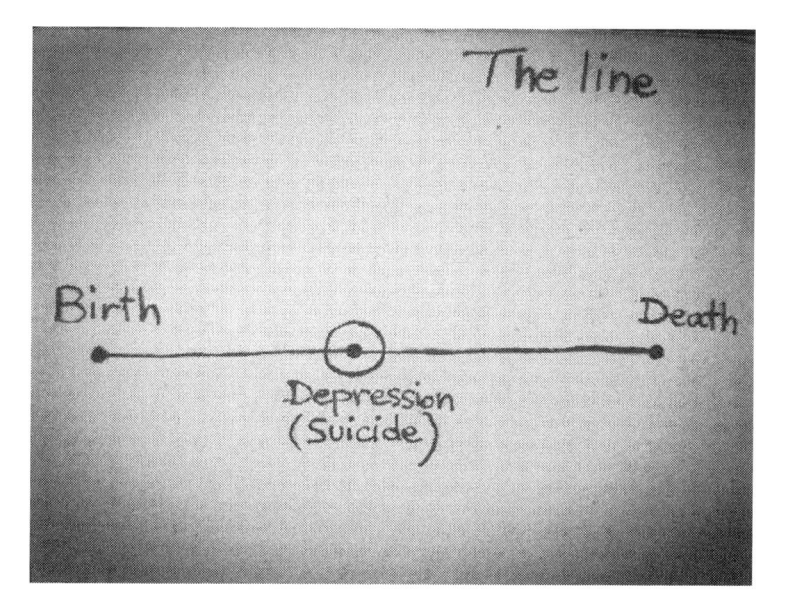

![The line — Birth ——— Depression (Suicide) ——— Death]

This refers to a vision of low level consciousness that determines the mental illness of the mind. In this 'Vision' the man sees himself projected on a road where there is a starting point (birth) and a point of departure (death). Halfway between birth and death, in many cases, the man gets involved in severe depressive crises that induce in him the desire for self-destruction that often results in suicide as a solution for not having to face old age and then death. It is seen in this case as the Ephemeral ending of a sad journey made not from your own choice but from such a frustrating and depressing cause that induces the confusion of mental illness.

'The Second Vision' was 'THE CIRCLE'

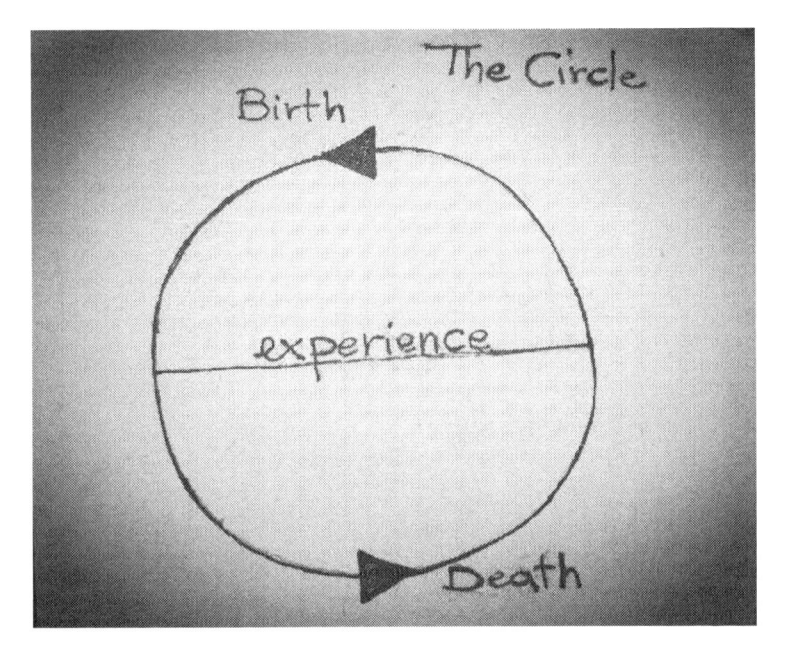

The Circle
Birth
experience
Death

This is a higher (upgraded) level view of Life than 'The Line' and is characterised by the awareness that death does not exist as a matter of fact but it is only a phase of a cycle in which man is destined to live an existence of birth and death, many times over. In the interaction between one cycle and another there is only one experience characterised by the essence of the cycle itself; that if it is not assimilated well can cause a 'Disease of the Soul'.

The person in this case realises that he is a prisoner in an interminable cycle of birth-death where their life is nothing more than the reoccurrence of cause-effect until there is progress in the level of consciousness that puts an end to the chaos in which things are repeated endlessly. The person in this case is comparable to a child who in school does not want to learn the lessons which he has continually failed and therefore must repeat the same school course until he learns it and so this is a level of consciousness that is quite frustrating because the person in this case (unlike the first where there is a complete clouding of the mind) realises his responsibilities that cause increasingly anxious states that give rise to the disease of the soul.

'The Third Vision' was 'THE SPIRAL'

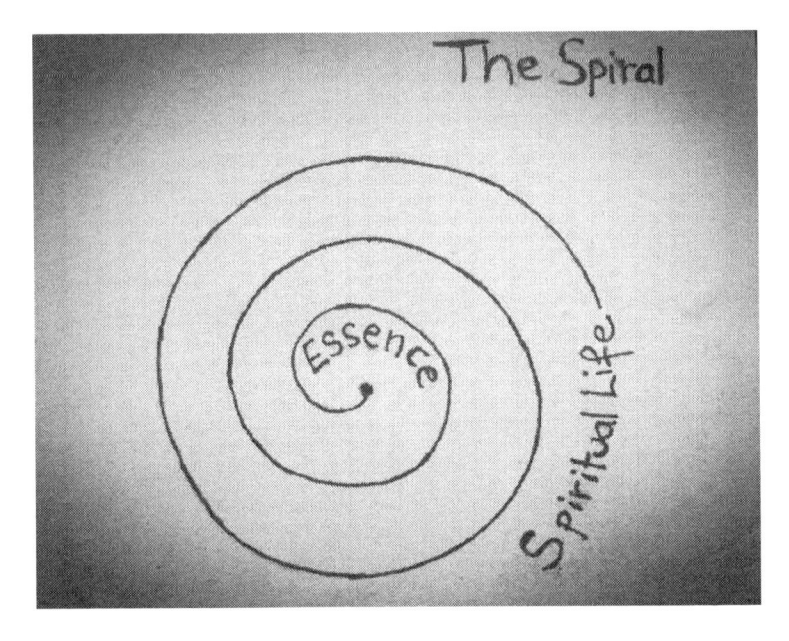

![The Spiral - a spiral diagram labeled with "Essence" at the center and "Spiritual Life" along the outer curve]

This is the vision of 'Christ Consciousness': the full awareness of one's own essence. The cycle of repeated lives and deaths is conceived as the path of purification that leads to the font of light (pure energy-essence), which is depicted as a spiral as the process speeds up through many lifetimes as one becomes closer to the essence–light). What comes from this kind of Vision is 'Joy'.

But that was not all: with the papyrus that described the 'Three Visions of Life' there was also a strange object which friar Sky had brought back with him. It was a small black container which was also sealed and from the secret place and therefore had to be a very important object. It was described fully in Elizabeth's diary. The three tried to figure out what it was. When friar Sky touched it he pushed one of the hemispheres set on it's surface which seemed to a be a simple blue stone set for a solely decorative purpose.

One of these stones however, was the key that allowed the bottom of the box to open and it contained a crystal which was half black and half white resembling the symbol of Tao with further symbols written on it in the same language of the Masuriti. Friar Sky hastened to read it while the other two tried to interpret the content by observing the increasingly surprised expression that was on the face of friar Sky.

"What is it about?" asked Alex, more anxious than ever.

Friar Sky had a moment's silence in which friar Sun and Alex both understood that it was something shocking.

Then friar Sky said "Yes, we have found the Secret of Life! This is the weapon described in Elizabeth's diary: 'The Holy Grail'. It's the most powerful weapon ever created on this planet. It is a nuclear device that has the power to destroy the world in a single moment. It was created to put an end to the destructive systems of the Black Masuriti, but from what I understand the people of the White Masuriti left it, so that whoever found it would have the option of choice as to whether to use it or not.

The diary says we can use it to give up the system and destroy the world or we can undo it by immersing it in the 'Waters of the Spring' source, a sacred place at the foot of the mountain from which flows a spring that comes from the mountain itself, flowing into an underground cave."

"And where is this Sacred place? Which mountain does the diary speak about?" asked Alex whilst looking around to try to figure out where the place could be.

"It is not here in Egypt" said friar Sky "It is in a small village in England called Glastonbury, not very far from London and in the middle of the country known to be a place of fairies and goblins. The people who live there have a strange air, perhaps for such a belief they still have an aspect that lies in mystery and magic. That's where we have to go to find the Holy Place."

It was then opening a new chapter of this intriguing history which would lead to the Holy Place where Alex and the two friars would face a new mystery that would lead them to England and precisely to Glastonbury.

26

THE BLACK MASURITI

The Investigation

Before they left Alex wanted to know more about Sarah's death so he got in touch with the Policeman who he knew, in the meantime, had been conducting investigations. But it was when he rang the Police Headquarters to ask to be put through to him that he was given the news that the Policemen was no longer in service and had withdrawn for unknown reasons.

Alex was surprised and didn't understand why the Policeman had left. He certainly hadn't warned him of his sudden decision. So Alex decided to get in touch with an old friend of his who, as far he remembered, was a Private Investigator specialising in archaeological finds who he knew from many years earlier at University. The man had been denounced many times for having published facts that had never been proved in which he claimed to be aware of political secrets manoeuvred by the elites of a high social class who obviously had no interest in being exposed publicly. But that young investigator had repeatedly tried to expose them without any result. Alex explained to him his current predicament:

"I hope you remember me" volunteered Alex "I'm a bit worried because I haven't been in touch for so long."

The man was John Fox and was based at the University of California where Alex had studied Archaeology. "I remember you. Yes, you were an ambitious young man looking for new things to discover and I'm not surprised that now you are involved in a sensational discovery. I swore you would make a career for yourself one day."

Alex felt relieved on hearing those words and suddenly found himself recalling those days as a student at the University where he loved to spend so much time deciphering the ancient symbols and phrases transcribed on old papyri and holy objects belonging to the ancient societies of people now disappeared. Only now was he realising that all those hours spent deciphering the past had distracted him away from the present and from his own life; the Here and Now that had only recently taken such importance in his mind.

Perhaps it was because what he was experiencing had, little by little, made him more aware of the 'Ultimate Reality' and was immersing him in what was, in the end, the purpose of that mission: to make light of reality from ourselves, to be at the centre of the cosmos as Beings of Light and then to expand as a Breath of God towards the confines of the Universe. This was the secret of living in the present, appreciating the value of the Here and Now as the only reality of our existence.

After wandering for a few moments in those memories of the past Alex returned to the main point by speaking to the young investigator again "I want to make you an interesting proposition that might be useful for your shocking publications."

"Sounds like exactly the kind of thing I'd be interested in" John answered "Tell me more."

"Good!" beamed Alex, pleased to have recruited such a skilful ally "A certain Police Officer called Roberto Pieraccini conducted investigations into the death of a certain Sarah Shiff and then mysteriously disappeared without a trace. I would like to know more: whether he's still alive and the reason he left the case."

With those words the young investigator was somewhat perplexed but the case was curious enough that he accepted Alex's proposal to investigate it. Alex sent him the file of his report so far, which included the information from the Police Officer and what hitherto seemed to be the result of his unconcluded investigation.

John Fox immediately began researching the root of the Society in his role of investigator and wanted to know what the content of the Congregation was. The old society founded previously by Elizabeth called "Esoteric Egyptian Society" gave details of their greatest enemy defined by the name of the 'Black Masuriti'.

"Who are these people who still live in the shadows today? And what are there intentions?" were just some of the questions already running through John's enquiring mind and in a very short time he had obtained the adrenaline needed that would allow him to quickly find the connections he needed for this story. This seemed to him to be a fairly difficult case but certainly not impossible.

The file presented information that the Congregation published periodically from the beginnings of it's foundation which were no longer possible to find on their website today. There were names published of suspected people connected to the financial companies such as banks and also to the nuclear weapons industries. These companies were actually those who apparently had the world's economic power in their hands but they hid secrets based on their esoteric knowledge about Energetic Alchemy as the sublime power of being able to manipulate the whole of humanity for global purposes which could be ultimately self-destructive.

The investigations continued for several days until John discovered that among the list of assorted names of those people stated as belonging to the Society of the 'Black Masuriti' there was one name of particular suspicion that reconnected to the Police Secret Service. It wasn't easy for John to discover this persons personal data but he finally managed to uncover a connection with archived data from the file of 'persons missing or presumed deceased' from which a name appeared that was very suspicious indeed.

27

THE SACRED PLACE

Glastonbury, England

The two friars and Alex thus departed for a new adventure. The one that would definitively conclude the mission that could save the Earth from irreparable disaster. When they arrived in Glastonbury they saw a seemingly quiet place frequented by curious tourists in search of mystery who came in and out of the shops full of gnomes and fairies, and magic trinkets and it was difficult to distinguish the reality from the fantasy especially in a speculative way, where the images become part of an economic source that feeds a whole community for generations.

There was no time to waste so they walked directly to the Waterfall of Purifying Water, the Sacred Place indicated in the papyrus. When they arrived at the entrance to the cave known as 'The White Spring' they were amazed by its apparent simplicity. It was semi-hidden by the rocks that were adorned with green moss from which oozed here and there small trickles of fresh spring water. Above, there was an ancient Tor that was originally a Sanctuary, and it dominated the hill; dedicated to Mother Earth, in honour of the Gods and Goddesses who represented her.

Inside the cave were representations of various figures of Divinity. The mysterious atmosphere was enveloped in a ritual where the spirit of Mother Earth was contemplated and respected, according to the traditional rules of and ancient Pagan culture. The environment was in twilight, lit only by candles scattered everywhere, almost to mark a path that led to a large basin between the rocks, in which flowed the water coming from the natural waterfall spring at the top of the hill. Inside the basin were three young, semi-clad women who, when they saw the three men enter, were preparing to welcome them, and one of them stepped forward saying:

"You've arrived, welcome! We have been waiting for you. We are the Goddesses of the Sacred Virtues: Youth, Joy and Compassion."

Friar Sky silently handed over the dark casket containing the secret weapon, instinctively knowing that this was the place described in Elizabeth's diary. One of the women took the object, and gently brought it into the basin where the other two women were waiting.

Then they put the device into the bottom of the basin and joined together in a circle and began to sing. Their voices spread through the cave with a divine sound and it tuned exactly with the sound of the running water, blending harmoniously together.

The three men were enchanted and were observing the scene in complete silence when they saw coming up from the bottom of the tub, a glowing light that slowly spread upwards as the intensity of the sound increased, then the three women suddenly plunged down into the water until they disappeared. The three men became anxious when they didn't see the women returning to the surface but they all noticed the outline shapes of their bodies spreading outwards with the light as their song still wafted through the air, until it too disappeared, leaving only the crashing sounds of the active waterfall inside the cave.

Then a woman's voice aroused them from their spell. She stood by the entrance, inviting them to join her outside saying:

"Come towards the light. The Planet Earth is safe now."

The woman wore a long brown robe, the colour of the Earth and she had a stick made from the branch of a tree on which she leaned. It symbolised the power of Nature and the woman, no longer young, had a serene face and large eyes filled with light and wisdom.

Her long silver-grey hair framed her beautiful face, giving her the appearance of Mother Earth. The three men approached her reverently. She was in the twilight at the doorway that led outside the cave. Outside the sun was shining brightly and before the three men left the woman told them:

"This is the beginning of a New Age in which humanity will be enlightened by a New Consciousness, which shall open their hearts and lead them to 'Eternal youth' that will manifest itself through the child spirit, towards 'Compassion and Solidarity' and therefore to 'Joy' as a result of their actions.

The water is the source. It is now purified with the transformation of negative energy into positive (Alchemy: the explosive device into the Holy Grail) and now it flows through the rivers and seas of this planet, purifying the souls of those who will bathe in it, and they will drink it in the sign of love for Christ and his precious blood which was given to us for peace.

The device was created in order to give humanity the choice between good and evil. They could destroy the Planet Earth in a single moment by the work of the Black Masuriti but at the same time they could save her by the work of the White Masuriti giving the instructions on how to undo the explosive effect, by cancelling it with its dissolution in the waters of this Blessed Spring.

Then the woman offered the three men a jug of water inviting them to drink a sip of it. The water had a bright and incandescent appearance and it tasted like the roots of the Earth at the moment of its flowering. It was the symbol of rebirth and after drinking it the three men realised they had an immediate transformation of their level of consciousness and acquired a clear awareness of their being in the depths of their essence:

Friar Sun became aware of his Vital Energy (Planetary Motion), friar Sky the way back home (The Milky Way) and Alex, the Messiah (The One Who Unites Men to Their Own Spirit). Then without saying another word they headed towards the exit, greeting the woman with a smile and the knowledge that their journey had ended. The three men remained silent from the moment they left the cave to the time when they re-entered Dendra Temple where they vanished between the columns, returning to that dimension which welcomed their return as if to their own home; letting the men of the Earth make their own spiritual path to freedom and knowledge of their own virtues.

28

THE INVESTIGATION

The Orion Sect

'Commissioner Sergio Leoni' was an important name on the list of alleged followers of the Sect called 'Orion'. This group was founded in 1820 by Artur Bauer, a German anarchist exponent, who in some of his manuscripts had several times revealed that he had extrasensory contacts which allowed him to access the occult powers coming from the 'Black Masuriti' dynasty from which he also originated.

The Orion Sect still had about eighty Adepts as members who all assumed false names in order to remain anonymous. They were all leaders of large corporations that included military, intelligence services, chemicals, banking and industrial services involved in the production of nuclear weapons.

Commissioner Sergio Leoni was a high ranking man who had made a career in the Police and upon retiring continued to perform duties on behalf of the CIA but his name had never been made public since he became a Secret Agent.

John Fox managed to track down the man who, by now very old, was living in an area of the Casentino nestled between the leaves of some fine olive trees and apparently living as a simple peasant now; tired of the hard work and devoted only to long walks in the green of nature.

John had the simple idea of contacting him for an interview by presenting himself as a Journalist of a magazine which focused primarily on the countryside and its produce. John had written for them before so the cover story could be verified.

The ageing Sergio didn't seem to worry that the Journalist could actually be a fake and had decided at the great age of 87 years that the time had come for him to take a well-deserved rest from the world that had seen him as the instigator of stories of high tension for so many years, and now an innocent interview dedicated to nature seemed like a beautiful ending.

It was a hot, spring afternoon when John arrived at the foot of the hill overlooking the cultivated lands of Casantino adorned with neat rows of olive trees and vineyards as if they were the decorating ornaments of a big wedding cake with Sergio's beautiful house on top, the cherry on the cake that now welcomed visitors with armoured security systems, almost indicating an extreme fear for its safety in complete contrast with the serenity of the environment.

"Good morning mister Leoni" said John Fox, cheerfully presenting himself with that dazzling smile that he normally adopted in an attempt to make a good first impression.

The old man was tall and distinguished and wore a huge cowboy-style hat that covered his eyes and most of his face.

"Good morning to you mister....?"

"John Fox is my name. I'm a journalist from the American magazine called 'Earthly Produce'." He held out his hand and the old man took it in his frail one and gave it a friendly squeeze.

The elderly man then granted him a smile and with a gesture of his waving arm invited him to go inside his villa, which was only a few tens of metres from John's parked car.

The Avenue that skirted the hill and led to the front door had post mounted security cameras that were slowly moving, to spy on anyone who made the slightest noise. The gate was heavily built and had a structure that unfortunately reminded John of a prison in Auschwitz. The interior of the house looked quite cosy but it breathed an uncomfortable atmosphere like someone was still watching them from small holes placed in the massive walls.

Sergio invited John to sit on a comfortable couch in the corner of the room and after offering him a lemon-based aperitif, that he described having made with some passion, he sat down in a comfortable armchair near the fireplace which, despite the warm autumn day, was always a pleasure for him; a blaze of fire that warmed his moments of solitude.

It took several minutes before Sergio began to talk about his life in retirement and despite the precise inquisitorial questions, Sergio seemed to easily dodge any answers that would have leaked his past, when he suddenly seemed to change his mind and for some reason the conversation headed into a completely different field that was in total contrast to what had been the original purpose of the interview.

"What really pushed you to move here, after having had a life and career in the military, full of responsibility?" asked John at one point; the young diplomatic investigator feeling secretly proud of his excellent investigative work.

"I understood that my past life was no longer important since I lost my wife. She died of sadness after the dramatic news of the death of our only son, who committed suicide after being part of a military mission during the Gulf War."

John was astounded by this news and understood then that this story was leading to some dramatic memories from the old man's past.

"That morning my son did not want to get up. He suffered from depression for a long time since he came back from the Gulf War where he had seen young people of his age dying next to him. He was only nineteen years old when he left for the war mission and after that traumatic experience he never recovered.

He had tried to keep his family together, but it didn't work, and after the inevitable divorce he decided that it was time to die. And so that morning he took the car and disappeared for several hours and was later found dead near a lake, not very far from home. He'd killed himself with the exhaust from the car. He was just a little over twenty-eight years old."

The elderly Sergio was evidently stirred by deep emotions and his sad eyes struggled to hold back the tears that lit up in the twilight of the room.

"I am very sorry. It is a very sad story but it is so important" said the young investigator, feeling upset by the narrative.

"And that's how, a few years after my sons death, my wife was diagnosed for severe heart dysfunctions and died as well. So I decided to retire from my military career to come here and meditate on nature and I started to see things I'd never seen, and hear things I'd never heard."

At this point John felt ready to open a new chapter which would bring the old man to talk some more "What do you know about the Orion sect?" he ventured.

"The Orion sect was an illusion and was created on basics that were destined to fail" said Sergio with an air which at this point sounded resentful. "There are people from this community who still believe they can control the world but still haven't understood that the values of life are not measured by ones power of control over others, but by the respect shown for nature and oneself."

These wise words of the older man had the air of being the product of years of profound meditation in which he himself had completely reversed, not only his life and thoughts, but also his vital energy and it seemed that this old 'Black Masuriti' adept had converted himself to the 'White Masuriti'.

"And what about the Masuriti?" asked the investigator, at this point sure that the older military man was ready to confess the unconfessable.

"Personally I don't know that much about the Masuriti but I read a long time ago, in the transcripts that define the laws regulating the community of Orion, that the ancient Egyptians were the proponents of these people who arrived mysteriously on the planet Earth, without traces of their provenance, a people who mysteriously appeared in Egypt some thousands of centuries ago.

It is said that it is divided into two sections: the 'Black Masuriti' and the 'White' one and that the 'Black' one brought the darkness, a symbol of evil as the consequence of their lack of love and light."

The investigator felt that the story had finally turned sufficiently for him to broach the real point of the matter: the mystery of Sarah's death.

"Do you know the Police Officer called Roberto Pieraccini?" asked the investigator. The question arrived like lightening in the clear sky.

And at that question the face of the elderly Sergio changed its expression and seemed somewhat troubled "I don't know him directly but I know he was in contact with someone in charge of the Orion Sect. I know he worked in their Secret Service but without being an active part of their community. He was a simple career Policeman who had been promised rewarding promotions that would bring him up to a higher level if he executed orders from the leaders of the Orion Sect."

Now is the moment, thought John "What happened to Sarah Shiff? Who killed her?" he demanded.

At this point Sergio became very agitated and upset, and standing up, moved to throw out the young investigator.

"Now that's enough! You came here with the excuse of interviewing me about nature and then ask me things about the secret service!? Who are you? You're a crook and a liar, and that's enough to ask you to get out of my house immediately!"

John Fox did his best to calm him down and hastened to explain the reason for his intrusion offering his apologies for disguising his true identity "I am sorry I troubled you with my intrusion" said the young investigator "But I think the time has come to avenge the death of your son who, through you, finally has the opportunity to shout for justice.

The war was certainly not what your son wanted but at the time he couldn't have known what was hidden behind it's false reality. War has never brought benefits to Planet Earth, and the Orion Sect is based on nuclear weapons control that even today, many of them produce, to enslave people just as in Antiquity they turned the Masuriti 'Black' after darkening their planet; which also darkened their hearts, making them arid and thirsty for vengeance."

Sergio calmed himself down and as his anger subsided, he re-seated himself and after inhaling deeply and slowly, he continued to speak:

"Sarah was a young warrior of peace but she bothered many people within the Orion Sect. She seemed to be informed about how to discover the secret, kept hidden for hundreds of centuries, that gave the possibility for Black Masuriti to someday have absolute power on Planet Earth. No-one knows what actually lurked inside this secret, but it is certain that Sarah was holding a potential power to reach that secret."

"She also had a diary written by an ancestor called Elizabeth" said the investigator "But what I want to know is who killed her" he continued determinedly.

"Roberto Pieraccini." revealed Sergio suddenly in a quiet voice "But he was just a pawn they were manipulating for their purposes, and he was paid very well to kill Sarah."

"And how did it happen?" asked John Fox.

"As far I know, that day after she arrived at the front of the monastery to meet a good friend, she was assaulted by an operator sent by the Police Officer, Pieraccini. He was a man from the East, in need of money, who killed her by choking her on behalf of the Officer." Sergio explained.

"And where is Officer Pieraccini right now?" asked the investigator.

"I don't know, but if it's true I believe he has been transferred to some country where he can live in anonymity in order not to be traced. But he might even have been killed after the fact to ensure his silence, the way the Sect usually do" the elderly Sergio ended, now tired of recalling the past.

"Thank you for your co-operation mister Leoni. And now let me say 'Goodbye' and take this trouble away from you. I wish you to live serenely and with the rest of your life in contact with nature."

John Fox then walked away from the old man who was sitting, staring into the diminishing flames that were still flickering in the fire place. Then he walked towards the car, taking one last look at that beautiful hill where time seemed to have stopped in search of the quiet, after the storm.

The investigator suddenly felt triumphant with his success and once he reached his studio he hastened to call Alex. But he never got any information. The phone was disconnected and the operator said:

"This number is unknown and the name Alex Tarantino never existed."

29

DENDRA

Elizabeth

It was a beautiful sunny day, and among the columns of the Temple of Dendra some tourists were wandering, when they heard in the distance the voice of a man and a woman calling for their little girl:

"Elizabeth where are you? Elizabeth!?"

They seemed very worried, when finally they heard the voice of the little girl running towards them who said:

"Mummy! Daddy! Look what I found!"

The little girl was holding a carefully tied papyrus. The parents did not pay much attention to the piece of paper, but rather to the little girl, that they thought they had lost forever among the pillars of the Temple; as they heard tell of, in some of the popular beliefs of that place. The three rushed out of the Temple and began looking for a place to sit for a short break.

While Mum and Dad were relaxing the little Elizabeth opened the papyrus where she found written:

"The Three Visions of Life: The Line, The Circle, The Spiral" and for each a brief explanation of the meaning.

Then at the bottom their was a brief postscript:

"Every Vision is the right way to return to your home where you will find yourself and you will understand who you are."

Then there was a poem entitled 'The Temple of Life':

"We are not rigid separate things, but fluid elements in continuous vibration; like cells of the same blood, we are moving into the river of life, carrying with us nourishment for one body that encloses us all as pillars of the same temple."

On the right hand side of the base of the papyrus were three names, each with their meaning: Sun (Vital Energy) Sky (Milky Way back to Home) Messiah (The Spirit's Message)

Elizabeth could hardly read the writing due to her young age, so she failed to fully understand the contents of the papyrus, but in her heart she knew that this was a precious asset which she kept inside a box along with other things that she held dear, and one day she will discover again to give her a Vision of Life and the way to go....

She never read the papyrus to her parents, but returning from that holiday she told her mum and dad that one day she would like to be an Archaeologist.

30

LUNIA

The Story

It's a lovely sunny day and in a small village in the Italian countryside a thirty three year old woman called Lunia is just finishing writing the last chapter of a story from her diary. She gets up and goes to her bedroom window where she sees a man and a woman arguing in the distance.

"Is this the beginning of a new adventure?" thinks Lunia, but the two people arguing this time are her mum and dad.

And as she watches them she smiles, understanding that she doesn't need to escape any more from reality into dreams of new adventures. Now she finally accepts the reality by forgiving her parents from the past, understanding the role of the circle of life where we become parents and then the difficulties of life especially when no Princes have arrived to rescue.

She finally concluded the last chapter of the story when a little voice called to her:

"Mummy! Can you come and play with me?"

"Yes Elizabeth, and I will also tell you a story called 'The Third Vision'."

THE AUTHOR

Giovanna O'Halloran-Bindi

Giovanna is an esoteric Italian woman who was born in Florence in 1963.

After studying Art at College she spent time as an Artist, Art Teacher, Graphic Designer and Puppeteer before focusing on Energy Work as a Therapist.

Her esoterically themed paintings have been exhibited in Italy and are also available on-line: giolandart.blogspot.com

She lives and works in London, running her own company 'Kalmatherapies' with her husband, Hypnotherapist Noel O'Halloran-Bindi who helped with suggestions and also translating and editing the English version from the Italian original, whilst retaining as much of the beautiful Italian prose as possible.

She regularly participates in Poetry and Performance groups and provides healing and insight for clients using crystals, singing bowls, gongs and her own distinctive style of massage in the London area. She has one son Christian Bernini who also lives in London.

Printed in Great Britain
by Amazon